Professed

Professed

A Novel of Higher Education

Lowell Mick White

Buffalo Times Press

AUSTIN

Cover Art: *The Machine,* by Reji Thomas
Author Photograph: Reji Thomas
Book Design: BTP

Library of Congress Cataloging-in-Publication Data

White, Lowell Mick, 1958-

   Professed : a novel of higher education / By Lowell Mick White.

      pages cm

   Summary: "A satire of academic life""[summary]"-- Provided by publisher.

   ISBN 978-1-943306-03-9 (pbk. : alk. paper) 1. Education, Higher--Fiction. 2. Teachers--Fiction. I. Title.

   PS3623.H57865P76 2013

   813'.6--dc23

                        2013020798

For

Glen Lowell White, PhD
1929-1976

and

Carol Mick White, PhD
1933-1988

Professors

The price one pays for pursuing any
profession or calling is an intimate
knowledge of its ugly side.
—James Baldwin

...abruptly Presley saw again, in his
imagination, the galloping monster, the
terror of steel and steam, with its single eye,
cyclopean, red, shooting from horizon to
horizon; but saw it now as the symbol of a
vast power, huge, terrible, flinging the echo
of its thunder over all the reaches of the
valley, leaving blood and destruction in its
path; the leviathan, with tentacles of steel
clutching into the soil, the soulless Force,
the iron-hearted Power, the monster, the
Colossus, the Octopus.
—Frank Norris

Professed

Professed

Fate

A man's power is hooped in by a necessity,
which, by many experiments, he touches on
every side, until he learns its arc.
—Ralph Waldo Emerson

At the end of the semester, the week after a cheerless and lonely Thanksgiving, on a dreary, rainy day, I was trudging along with mobs of young students through Parlin Hall, the English building, when someone called my name. I looked around. Damp, dripping students were coming and going in the hallway, many chattering chatting chatting on cell phones, some hooked up to headphones listening to music, jostling along with backpacks and books. Then I saw Dr. Camille Braddock, a professor I'd had in graduate school.

"Tom!" she said. "What luck—I was just thinking about you."

I felt a sudden wave of guilt and anxiety. She had no reason to be thinking about me. I asked, "What?"

Dr. Braddock stepped between a pair of giggling girls and came over. She was dry—had probably been teaching in one of the classrooms upstairs—and trim and cheerful, carrying an armload of multicolored folders. Student work, probably: even professors had to grade, sometimes, a little.

"Absolutely," Dr. Braddock said. "I was thinking about you—wondering if you might be able to do me a favor."

A favor. I looked away, down the hall to the retreating

girls—still giggling, and it briefly occurred to me to wonder just what the hell they were so happy about—and I then looked back at Dr. Braddock. It was one of those day-to-day moments that everyone has at times, I think, and seem to happen to me fairly regularly, moments that open up into an eternity, an endless unfillable void where a person can instantly pause to consider just how screwed-up a life can become. A favor. I was already doing too much, and following through on too little. I was a post-doc, a lecturer, an adjunct—a debt-slave, a serf. I was teaching two sections of Intro to Literature and a section of Composition and Rhetoric at the university, and three sections of comp at the community college. I was tending bar three nights a week to get enough extra money to at least make payments on my loans. I was scrambling around trying to find a tenure-track job. And Dr. Braddock, who should have known or at least sensed my status and situation, wanted to ask me for a favor.

"A favor?" I asked. I was starting to come up out of the void, and I was pissed, and depressed.

A fucking favor.

"You have a minute?" Dr. Braddock asked. "Or do you have to go teach?"

I checked my watch. I had twenty minutes until the next class. "No, I'm free right now."

"Excellent—come on to my office."

I turned and followed Dr. Braddock up the hallway I had just come down. The floor was a little muddy and slippery from all the water the wet students had tracked in, but Dr. Braddock calmly stepped along in an expensive pair of black boots. Faculty offices opened on either side of the hall: the office doors had large, frosted glass windows in them, and many professors had photos and newspaper clippings taped to their doors—cartoons, funny sayings, poems. Dr. Braddock's door, though, was bare: creamy whitish gray paint, the frosted gray window, a cardboard tag with her name and office hours. Over the years I'd been past this door dozens of times, maybe hundreds, but had never gone through it, not even when I was one of her students.

"Come on in," Dr. Braddock said. She unlocked the door and opened it. "Have a seat."

Dr. Braddock's desk faced the door, and beyond it was a window—a window! My office, if you could even call it that, was stuck in the dark dungeon-like basement of the under-graduate library, a dank cubicle I shared with a pair of ad-juncts from the Spanish department and a leaky sewage pipe. Dr. Braddock's office was big and dry and had a window. Life on the tenure track! I almost felt like crying.

"Sit down, please." Dr. Braddock dumped her big armload of student work to the desktop. A red folder slipped off onto my side of the desk, and I picked it up and put it back. I sat down. I waited to hear about the—favor.

"Just a second," Dr. Braddock said. "There's something I need to look at."

Well. Sure. Make the serf wait. Life on the tenure track. I sat back while Dr. Braddock checked her email. There were bookshelves on either side of the desk, and behind the chair I was sitting in. I recognized a few titles: Goetzmann's *West of the Imagination*, Nash's *Wilderness and the American Mind*. *Desert Solitaire, Great Plains, Regionalism and the Humanities*. Dr. Braddock worked in literary and photo-graphic narratives of the American West.

"So—how are you?" Dr. Braddock turned away from her computer and looked at me. "You're lecturing, right? On the job market?"

"Yeah," I said. "I interviewed at Southeast Kansas State a couple of weeks ago."

"Southeast *Kansas*," she said, slowly. There was a little trace of—what? Mockery? Pity?—in her voice, like she was really saying *Bumfuck* State or something. What the hell—Southeast Kansas was a real job, with health insurance. It couldn't be that bad. She asked, "How'd that go?"

"Haven't heard anything yet," I said.

"It's rough out there," Dr. Braddock said. "The job market's tight."

I shrugged. "That's what everybody says."

"I know you'll find something good," Dr. Braddock said. "But listen—I wanted to ask you for a favor."

Finally. I asked,"Yeah?"

Dr. Braddock leaned forward like she was about to share a secret. Her chair squeaked.

"I'm going out to California over break," she said. "I'm going to do some work at the Bancroft Library and I was wondering—thinking—hoping—that maybe you could come by and feed the cats while I'm gone."

"The cats?" I asked. I slumped down a little in the chair.

I thought, At least cats are less trouble than dogs.

"Yeah, my cats, they need somebody to come by a couple of times a day and feed them. It shouldn't be too much trouble—they're older cats."

The void opened up again. Despair seeped out.

I do too much, I don't follow through enough. It was the end of the semester: in a few days I would have 150 or so papers to grade and a job search to organize. A life to lead. Despair seeped out of the void, enveloped me. I was going to say Yes, of course I was—I couldn't say No, ever. My parents raised me to be nice, to be agreeable, to be helpful, and I am. It's a quality that has never served me well. When friends need help moving, I move. When students think their grade is too low, I raise the grade. Dentists and doctors schedule my appointments at weirdly inconvenient times. Butchers sell me bad meat. I paid too much for my car, and pay mechanics too much for not fixing it. I can't say No. If I was a girl, I'd be pregnant all the goddamn time, with a half-dozen or so brats from previous favors—previous Yeses—squalling around unfed in dirty diapers. It's just the way I am. When I look in the mirror I see a very weak man.

"Yeah, I guess," I said. The void closed. The despair, I knew, would linger. "I mean—sure. I don't have any plans or anything. I like cats."

"Excellent!" Dr. Braddock said. "I knew you were the man for the job!"

From: Emily Caldwell
To: Thomas Holt, PhD
Subject: Money

So when are you going to get me that money for the
electric bill? This is taking way too long!

Emily!

At two o'clock on Monday and Wednesday and Friday
afternoons, I taught a class over in Garrison Hall, a section of
RHE 306, Rhetoric & Writing, and it was the class I always
dreaded—not so much for the class itself, 25 or so sullen
young people who didn't want to be there, but for the room I
taught in. Garrison 128 was right next door to Garrison 132,
and in Garrison 132 at 2:00 MWF was a class taught by my
ex-girlfriend, Emily Caldwell.

I did my best to avoid Emily, but even so I managed to
run into her at least once a week before or after class. Seeing
her was always the low point of my week. Emily was always
quick with a snarky remark about someone or something—
bad professional behavior, I thought—and even quicker to
bug me about money she claimed I owed her on our last
electric bill.

In order to avoid Emily I usually got to Garrison 128 a
few minutes after the class was scheduled to start—Emily
of course was always very punctual and always began her
classes on time. I was happy to dodge her and begin class a
few minutes late, much to the annoyance of a few students
who saw themselves as consumers of education and expected
the university to be as smoothly run as a goddamned Jiffy-
Lube. I was unmoved by the consumers, though, and usually
ended class a few minutes early, too, rushing the students
out into the hall and off to wherever they had to go, then
fleeing myself. I put more work into dodging Emily than I did
teaching the class.

But after seeing Dr. Braddock I was running a bit later
than normal, even, and to cover the material I ended up

running the class longer than usual, too, aware of the few students who were angry at me for my weird starting and stopping times, and the many students who were pissed because I hadn't finished grading the essays they'd turned in almost three weeks earlier. Still, class came to an end, and the students dropped off their homework assignments and bustled off into the hall. I could see through the open door that Emily's class was letting out, too. I scrambled around, trying to pile up everything—homework, handouts, whatever—so I could escape. When I looked up again, I saw a student coming back into the room—Nelda Krueger, a pretty girl who had been making me nervous all semester.

"Dr. *Holt*," Nelda said.

I looked past Nelda and saw Emily standing in the doorway.

"What can I do for you?" I asked. I looked away from Nelda, down at the jumbled stack of paper on my desk.

"I was wondering what the deal was on the final portfolio," Nelda said. She had fine brownish blondish hair and sharp brown eyes and pearly teeth and she smiled with her wet mouth open. "You said it was supposed to be our best paper, revised, but I haven't got my last paper back yet, and it's my best one, I think. So how can I revise it if I don't know what you think of it?"

"There's plenty of time," I said. Emily was still standing in the doorway, clutching books to her chest and pouting. I looked back at Nelda. "I'll get the papers back Wednesday— or maybe Friday, or Monday—and you'll have plenty of time for revision."

Nelda put her hand on the table and looked distressed. "But I have all these other assignments coming due! You know? I'd like to get this one out of the way."

"You're going to have plenty of time," I said again. "Really—you're doing fine in this class. You don't have anything to worry about."

"Okay." Nelda didn't sound convinced.

"Come by my office and talk to me," I said. "We'll get it

worked out for you. You're going to do fine."

"Okay," Nelda said again.

"Send me an email if you have any questions," I said.

"Thanks, Dr. Holt," Nelda said. She turned to leave and I watched her walk away, then looked up at Emily standing there, dumpy and frumpy and frowning. She came slowly over to my table.

"So," Emily said, "I guess that's the student you're fucking this semester, huh?"

"What?" I looked at her. "No!"

"I saw how you looked at that girl," Emily said.

"What?" I asked. "I was not! Besides, what am I supposed to look at—the floor?"

Emily smiled a little. "You can look at anyone you want, as long as you look professionally."

Professionally. Right. I asked, "Yeah? So who are you fucking now?"

"Not a student!"

Somebody, then. I didn't care.

Emily said, "So, when are you going to get me that money for the electric bill?"

The electric bill. That. I sagged. "I don't have it," I said. "You'll have to wait."

"I've been waiting," Emily said. "It's not much."

I pulled out my billfold and gave her twenty dollars. I said, "That's all I have right now."

Emily stuck the bill in her pocket. "You still owe me eighty-four dollars."

"Whatever," I said.

Students from the next class were filtering into the classroom. I finally jammed the homework into my briefcase. I said, "I've got to get out of here."

I grabbed my briefcase and we left the room and went up the stairs and out onto the mall. The rain had stopped but the sky was still overcast and low. I started back toward my dungeon in the basement of the UGL.

"Walk me over to Parlin," Emily said. "I need to check

my mail."

"I was just over there," I said.

"Well, you can go again."

I gave up. We passed the statues of Jefferson Davis and Woodrow Wilson and down the steps to Parlin. Emily, still in grad school, had a mailbox there. Me, a post-doc, a nobody, an unperson with no rights, of course had nothing, nothing, anywhere.

"You shouldn't stare at your students like that," Emily said.

I shrugged and didn't say anything. Emily was always jealous. I remembered mornings when Emily would sit puffy-faced and grouchy, watching the cable news. The blond women reading the news always seemed to annoy her. "You'd probably fuck her, wouldn't you?" she asked one morning, pointing at the television with the remote.

I said, "I don't know."

"Of course you would. The valorization of blondness in this society is a disease."

I said, "Everybody on TV is beautiful."

"Her mouth looks like a vagina," Emily said.

Every morning was like that—one grouchy whine after another. Emily was very smart—sharper than me, at least—but her never-ending petulance made her a pain to be around. Really, I was happy when she kicked me out.

Just outside Parlin we passed a curly-headed little man all dressed in black.

"Hi, Dr. Wytowski," Emily said.

He walked on past us without looking up.

Emily leaned over to me. "Wytowski's wife left him. He's fucking a student, too."

"How do you know?"

"Everybody knows! Everybody's talking about it! The girl went on grademyprofessor.com and gave him straight fives and a chili pepper 'cause he's so hot."

I turned and looked at Wytowski walking away from us. I said, "He's not so hot."

"Well, you're not fucking him." Emily opened the mailroom door for me. "That girl thinks he's hot. She even gave him a double-t hott. And then his wife went online and gave him a frowny face—you can't get any lower than a frowny face—and she said he was a lousy lay."

The mailroom was decorated with photos of long-dead and forgotten professors. They made me sad, the photos of the forgotten dead, all gazing out at me with glittering professorial eyes. They made me feel like a loser, too—a loser who would never even get into a position to be forgotten, a loser who would never get to be a professor, a loser destined for an endless miserable adjunct life. Forget me later, I thought. Give me tenure now. At least give me health insurance now! Emily peered into her mailbox—nothing, of course, just a flyer for some lecture series nobody was interested in, and a memo reminding instructors to get their grades turned in on time. Emily dumped the papers into a recycling bin.

"Listen," Emily said. "I wanted to ask you a favor."

Another fucking favor—of course.

The void opened up again. But I tried to stop it.

"I already paid you what I have—"

"What you *owe* me is an obligation—"

"I don't have anything else—"

"This is a favor—"

"And I'm not sure I owe you anything!"

"A favor, okay? This won't cost you anything."

Sure. I looked at the photos of the dead professors and didn't say anything. They didn't say anything, either. A heavy-set, professorial-looking woman ducked into the mailroom and peered into her mailbox. She dumped some unread paper into the recycling bin and ducked back out.

"A favor," Emily said. "I was just thinking you could read a chapter of my dissertation."

Her dissertation. Oh, that. Right. It had something to do with gender roles in the anti-slavery movement, or maybe early feminists—rhetorical positions, something something whatever whoever. We'd talked a lot about her dissertation—

well, she talked a lot, and I pretended to listen—but even after three years I was never really clear about what she was working on.

"I don't have any time," I said. "I'm teaching six fucking classes. I have papers to grade."

"There's no real rush," Emily said. "A week or so, maybe."

"I'm too busy—"

"There's no one else I can hand this to," Emily said. "You're the Emerson expert."

"I am not!" My own work was on early 20th century environmental literature, mostly on the influences of John Muir, and though of course Muir and other nature writers were all heavily influenced by Thoreau and Emerson, and though of course I had read all those guys, I was certainly no expert.

Emily said, "You took that Transcendentalism Seminar."

"So did you!"

"Yeah, but you paid attention."

The void opened wider—really, really opened. I could feel my whole future falling into it, joining my past, which was of course already lost in shadowy hellish nothingness.

"C'mon," Emily said. "I'll buy you dinner."

Right, I thought. Buy me dinner with the money I pay you for the electric bill I don't owe anything on. But I didn't say anything. I still remembered Emily's prickliness, her defensiveness, her sincere aversion to any sort of criticism. In the Transcendentalism Seminar she'd written a paper on gender roles and transgression in *The Blithedale Romance*, and I'd made a couple of suggestions—just moving a couple of paragraphs around—and she didn't speak to me for a week.

"C'mon," Emily said. "It won't be so bad."

From: Cynthia Gaines, Assistant Director of Undergraduate Rhetoric and Writing
To: All Instructors
Subject: Grades

Instructors, this is just a reminder that you need to post

your grades to the system no later than 5:00pm, December 18. Late grades must be hand-delivered to the Registrar's Office.

Also, in this Holiday Season, I want to assure all of you that you are appreciated by the University, and the University Community.

Dr. Gaines

Grading was an ordeal for me. Six sections of 25 students, more or less, each student spitting out four papers over the course of a semester—600 papers of an overall dismally low quality, 3000 pages or so of the same errors, same lame punctuation, same irrational arguments. My hand got tired writing in the margins

SF

WC

UC

Sentence fragment, word choice, unclear. Over and over. What I wanted to write was

WTF

or

BS!

or

ZZZZZZZZZZZ!!!!!!

or even

YAS!!!!!!!!!!!!!!!!!!!!!!!!!!!!

What the fuck or ***bullshit*** or ***boring*** or ***YOU ARE STUPID!!!!!!!!!!!!!!!!!!!!!!!!!!!***
But I didn't.
Everybody I know hates grading. Even the instructors and professors who claim to love their students—and who actually may love teaching, after all—even they hate grading.

It's tough to judge and asses people and then look them in the eye day after day. Beneath that is a cold lurking fear of getting a bad evaluation from an unhappy student, a bad evaluation that can doom your career. One or two bad evaluations from terrible students can get a non-tenured faculty member's contract canceled, and the teacher can find her or his ass out on the street with no job, no job prospects, and $150,000 or so of student debt to pay off.

And still grading is worse than that, even—grading affects the health of teachers, too. Meet some afternoon with 14 or 18 students to discuss their terrible papers and you'll be sick the next day—students are notoriously filthy vectors of cold and flu viruses—and you'll be depressed, too, worried for the fate of the republic after you've read students who assert that their "mine is maid up" or that they are not taking something "for granite," or who argue that Hitler did some good things, like build roads (and, anyway, "It was God that judged the Jews"), or who are just plain lazy ("Both of these stories that I am comparing have similarities that me as a reader will know about when I finish reading them"). And I'm not kidding about the depression. Grade 30 or 50 papers and you will feel low, sullen, tired, you will feel like a loser, like a horrible teacher, like a total failure. The good papers— and yes, there are some good papers always—won't cheer you up because the bad papers are bad, bad, bad. They are terrible, and they're terrible because you're a terrible teacher. It's depressing. A year ago here an adjunct jumped off the west side of the football stadium and killed himself. His suicide note even made the *Chronicle of Higher Education*: he blamed grading for his depression—not lousy adjunct pay or not having health insurance. Grading. It's a killer.

The English Department and the overseers of freshman composition tried to help us—they claimed to try to help us, anyway. There were grade-norming workshops throughout the semester, though few people attended them (I never did), and they supplied us with a subscription to an online service called Chek-Student-Papers.com. CSP was many things—a full classroom management package—but the main thing it offered was a plagiarism detector. Students would upload their papers and the service would compare the student work with their database of a gazillion or so published articles and student papers. Many instructors thought there was something unethical about CSP: it was as if we were assuming that students were going to cheat, and by making that assumption we were violating a level of student-teacher trust. Maybe so. But the university required that we use it; so I used it.

And so I was checking my last batch of papers for my stupid 2:00 MWF class—papers I'd had for almost a month before getting around to even looking at them—when there was a dull little plooting bleep on my computer: one of the papers was coming up as 77% unoriginal material. 77%! The highest I'd ever seen. I clicked on link to the paper.

It belonged to Nelda Krueger, the cute little girl Emily had given me shit about. Cute little thief, I thought. Her paper attempted to argue that an obsession with high school football made Texas a unique place: "High School Football is part of the rich beautiful Tapestry that is Life in Texas."

I do an exercise in class where I have the students read their thesis paragraphs aloud, so the whole class can critique them, and I remembered Nelda reading that line in class. It made my heart sink so low I couldn't even tell her how to fix the damn thing. But now as I read on, past the first paragraph, the tone of the essay changed, and began to read like a movie review. Oh—and that's what it was, according to CSP, the entire body of the essay was taken from a review of the film Friday Night Lights that had been published years ago in Texas Monthly. When the review referred to characters in the movie, Nelda changed the names to "a player" or "some players" or "some coaches." That was it: a half-retarded thesis paragraph and three pages of a copied movie review, with no attribution, no works cited, no nothing.

And it *would* be her, too—Nelda, one of the few students I could recognize in class. I could recognize her, all right.

From the first day I'd noticed her. I'd been pacing around the front of the classroom, going over the syllabus or something equally stupid when I looked down and noticed a student's feet propped up on my desk. A girl student's feet—small, compact, encased in a pair of gray Nikes. A girl student slouched down in her seat with her feet up in my space. Right there, in class, on the first day, the void began to open up, and this time the void was linked to the lower parts of my brain, which was linked to all my other lower parts. I looked up past her sneakers and feet, looked up her sturdy brown sleek legs, up, up, all the way up to her crotch, where the girl's vulva was outlined in the tight yellow fabric of her shorts. Right there in class—on the first day—I stopped everything I was doing and stared at her pussy. The void opened up. I forgot what I was saying. I guess the other students picked up on my confusion, because after a while I sensed some restlessness in the classroom.

I blinked. "Uh, do you always sit with your feet up on the teacher's table?"

"I'm sorry." The girl straightened up and pulled her feet to the floor. Her crotch disappeared. "I just like to be comfortable."

"Well." I sighed. "Well, don't let me make you uncomfortable."

Though of course I was the one who was uncomfortable.

The next class she was slouched down again with her feet up. She was wearing different shorts, denim cutoffs, but I knew what was up there. All semester long she slouched, all semester long I was uncomfortable.

And now, at the end of the semester, she was still making me uncomfortable with a stupid fucking stolen paper. And more than making me uncomfortable, she was criminally complicating my life.

> From: Camille Braddock
> To: Thomas Holt, PhD
> Subject: Ben and Fred

Hi, Tom—I was just thinking that you could perhaps stop by my house tonight or tomorrow to meet Ben and Fred and let me show you around. My address is Six Arbor Ridge—it's off Westlake Drive (make sure you stay on Westlake and don't take the fork over the hill!) Give me a call and let me know when you're coming—

All Best,

Camille

Dr. Braddock's house was tucked away hidden in a new development in the hills west of town, and I had some trouble finding it—yes, I took the left-hand fork instead of the right one, and I went up over a dark, wet hill. I made a right somewhere and drove past the gates of enormous mansions. Some of the big houses were lit up for coming Christmas, lights peeping through thick trees. I got turned back around, went down the backside of the hill and ended up on Westlake, where I should have been in the first place, all twisty and turny in the dark. I didn't have GPS, and so I'd printed a map off the internet, and I had to stop a couple of times to look at it before I found the development, The Arbors at LakeRidge, a cluster of new homes set down along the top of a cliff. I found Arbor Ridge, a cul-de-sac, and Number Six—the numbers were spelled out on all the houses—at the very end. I parked the car and got out.

The houses fronted the street with walls and gates, and there didn't seem to be any life—any movement—around, except for water dripping from the oaks and cedars. I could smell woodsmoke in the air, and Dr. Braddock's steel gate felt cold when I pushed it open. A graveled path led up to her door.

A lit window faced me—a kitchen window, I thought, with warm light inside and frilly curtains, and movement of some sort. I almost turned and ran away. Almost said fuck it—fuck Dr. Braddock, fuck the cats, fuck the favor. But I didn't run away. I wanted to, but I didn't. I pushed on the glowing plastic doorbell, and the door opened immediately.

"Tom!" she said. "I've been looking for you. Come in!"

Dr. Braddock looked good: tight black sweater, black jeans, black and red ropers. She stepped aside, holding the door open, and as I stepped past her I caught the scent of her perfume, rich and bright.

"Did you have any trouble finding me?" Dr. Braddock asked. She was standing in the doorway, looking out through her gate to the street.

"Not really."

"It's so dark out here you can barely see the street signs! About half the time people come to see me, they drive right past the turnoff and end up on 360 or back in town."

"Or they take the wrong fork and go over the hill," I said. "It's an adventure—it's like being Lewis and Clark or something."

"Without a Sacajawea to show you the way," Dr. Braddock said. "How sad." She shut the door. "Well, this is the house."

"Beautiful home," I said. I looked around. There was a kitchen—the kitchen with the warm light—to my left, and a living room to my right. Once again I thought, Life on the fucking tenure track.

"Thanks—I'm so happy here." Dr. Braddock stepped past me again. "Let's introduce you to the boys. Fred! Ben!"

I followed her into the living room—nice, tasteful, fireplace with a popping little fire, bookshelves full of books, prints of 19th century photographs on the walls. Over the fireplace was a large Russell Chatham lithograph, a winter scene in the west somewhere, brown cattle standing in a snowy field with a horizontal gray band of river running across the background. A very quiet work.

"Here's Fred!" Dr. Braddock bent over and came up with an armful of yellow cat. "This is Fred. Fred, this is Tom."

Dr. Braddock came over and held Fred out, and I felt obligated to take the cat from her.

"I wonder where Ben is?" she asked.

I had no idea. Fred the cat lay stiffly still in my arms for a moment—he felt tense and cranky. Then he kicked me in the belly and twisted around and dropped to the floor. Fred walked over to the fireplace, then turned and sat and stared at me. I thought, Fuck you, Fred.

"Here's Ben!" Dr. Braddock motioned me over. "I don't want to disturb him."

I crossed the room and stood next to Dr. Braddock. There was an old gray striped cat dozing on the floor. He opened his eyes and looked sleepily up at us.

"Ben, this is Tom. He's going to be feeding you while I'm gone."

"Hey, Ben," I said. Ben closed his eyes again. I guess I'm not very impressive.

"He's old," Dr. Braddock said. "He sleeps a lot."

"Lucky Ben."

"Now, remember," Dr. Braddock said, "they're inside cats—they never go outside."

"Never?" I asked.

"Never," she said. "It's dangerous out there—they could get hit by cars, or attacked by coyotes. People lose cats and small dogs all the time."

"Damn."

Dr. Braddock led me back through the kitchen, gleaming and spotless, to what she called "the feeding nook," a little corner of the kitchen back near the walk-in pantry. There were four dishes on the floor, a water dish and food dish for each cat.

"The red ones are for Ben, and the black ones are for Fred," Dr. Braddock said.

"It makes a difference?"

"To them it does! They have very different feeding requirements—Ben's much older than Fred." Dr. Braddock nudged one of Ben's red bowls with the red toe of her boot. "Also, I think Fred prefers black—he's got a little Goth thing going on or something."

I looked back to the front of the house and saw both cats

watching me. I said, "Good for Fred."

"The litter boxes are down here."

I followed Dr. Braddock down a short flight of stairs. The house—like all the houses on the street, I guess—was hacked into the limestone edge of a ridge, and had a sort of semi-basement, unusual in Texas. At the foot of the stairs was a little room with the cat boxes—two pale green plastic boxes. I guess Fred's Gothic impulses didn't extend to where he crapped. Sliding glass doors led outside, and there were metal utility shelves crammed with textbooks along the walls. Through a doorway I could see another room with a washer and dryer. Everything smelled like lemon air freshener.

"Well, these are the boxes—you'll have to clean them frequently."

"Look at all the textbooks," I said.

"Oh, those." Dr. Braddock shrugged. "Publishers keep sending me exam copies of rhetoric texts—handbooks, readers, I don't know. Nothing I can use, though, and I don't want them cluttering up my office, so I end up lugging them home."

"You could sell them," I said. A couple of times a semester an odd-looking little man would wander through the adjunct dungeon buying up spare textbooks. And we always had them, too, even the Spanish instructors. As Dr. Braddock said, publishers were always sending out exam copies of their books. Selling them was a good way to make a few extra bucks.

"Too much trouble." Dr. Braddock picked up a box of trash bags. "These are for when you clean the litter box. Fresh litter is in the bin by the wall."

Dr. Braddock headed back up the stairs. I was right behind her, my face inches from her butt, tight in jeans. In class sometimes I would space out into fantasy, a more pleasant version of the void, wondering what she looked like naked, having my little fantasy while slides of Albert Bierstadt and Alfred Jacob Miller flashed on the walls around us.

"I'll send you an email with the details of the feeding and

cleaning," Dr. Braddock said over her shoulder. "It's pretty basic."

"I think I can handle it," I said. I was staring at her ass.

Ben joined us at the top of the stairs and followed us to the door. He was rubbing against Dr. Braddock's legs. Seemed like a nice cat.

"Well." Dr. Braddock looked at me. "Do you have any questions—about anything?"

I looked down at Ben. "No, I guess not."

Dr. Braddock laughed. "You never ask questions! I've noticed that about you."

I blushed. "I guess it's my learning style."

"Well, it obviously works." Dr. Braddock opened the door and put her hand on my arm. "Thank you so much!

> From: Thomas Holt, PhD
> To: Nelda Krueger
> Subject: Paper #4
>
> Hi Nelda,
> I've been grading your paper and I have some questions about it. Could you come see me before class Monday?
>
> Dr. Holt

.

> From: Nelda Krueger
> To: Thomas Holt, PhD
> Subject: re: Paper #4
>
> Oh yea I was having problems with the paper check thing I might have sent you the wrong paper do you want me to send you the right one?
>
> Nelda :)

My boss, such as I had one, was Dr. Cynthia Gaines,

Assistant Director of Undergraduate Rhetoric and Writing. I knew that the plagiarism report would flag to her office, so I sidestepped the void and showed a little initiative: I made an appointment to see her, before one of her minions got around to contacting me. And, really, I hoped I could throw the problem over to her office before I had to do anything about it.

I'd seen Dr. Gaines before—had heard her speak at the big meetings we'd have before the start of each semester—but I didn't know her at all. She was a tall, elegant black woman and seemed very tough.

"So, you've got a problem with a student," she said when I came into her office.

"Well, yeah," I said. I told her about the CSP plagiarism flag—the 77%—about the ease with which I was able to Google up the movie review Nelda had plagiarized. I handed Dr. Gaines some printouts: Nelda's essay with the stolen sections highlighted (nearly all of it), and a copy of the movie review, also with the stolen sections highlighted.

"It looks pretty bad," I said. "But—"

"It looks pretty bad," Dr. Gaines said. "Have you talked to the student yet?"

"I sent her an email immediately after I found—this." I didn't know what to call it—the plagiarism, the theft, the shit. "That was Friday night. I told her I needed to talk to her before or after class Monday. But she didn't show up to class. And then last night I got this."

I handed Dr. Gaines a copy of the email where Nelda said it was a mistake, that she'd uploaded the wrong paper.

Dr. Gaines read the email and then looked up at me. "And you believe her?"

"I don't know," I said. "About an hour ago she emailed me a new paper—everything's different, she doesn't even use the same source material, and everything's cited."

Dr. Gaines looked over the printouts, and sighed. After a moment, she asked, "So, when was this paper due?"

"The nineteenth," I said. I felt stupid. Also afraid that she might ask me why it was taking me over three weeks to grade the damn papers.

"November the nineteenth," Dr. Gaines said, slowly. She thought for a moment. "And today's December fourth. So this girl's had two extra weeks to get her paper together, right? And four days since she got caught."

I said, "Well...."

"And she says it was a mistake."

"Yeah."

Dr. Gaines said, "We've had seventeen mistakes like that in the past two weeks, people claiming they turned in the wrong paper."

"Damn!"

"Even if it is a mistake, it's her responsibility to turn in the correct paper on time."

"Sure," I said.

"So what do you want to do about it?"

Over the weekend I'd been mad at Nelda—mad, offended, pissed—not only had she violated the trust that is supposedly so important in the classroom, she was causing me to do extra work. Extra work, and I didn't have time to do my regular work. I was pissed. But then when I got the revised paper, I kind of believed her, believed that she had actually maybe learned something in my class, that she had merely made a mistake, really, that she really did know how to cite sources, that she knew that lifting texts was wrong. That she was honest. Over the weekend I had wanted to give her an F, fail her in return for the extra work she was making me do, the grading, the printing, the highlighting, the fretting. Hell, I wanted to give her an F-minus, I wanted her expelled from the university! But now—

"Well," I said. "Even if it was a real mistake, the correct paper was turned in late."

"A month late," Dr. Gaines said.

"So she's going to get an F either way." I felt relieved. I didn't really have to make a decision.

"You can go so far as to award her an F for the entire

course," Dr. Gaines said. "Or you can require her to take Scholastic Integrity Counseling. Or you can turn her over to the Academic Review Board—they might even expel her. Basically, though, it's up to you. You can give her whatever you want."

"I don't know," I said.

Dr. Gaines looked at me and frowned. I looked away. After a moment she asked, "Aren't you angry about this?"

"Well, yeah."

"I'd nail her, myself," Dr. Gaines said.

I sat up a little bit. "Well, then, let's nail her." Fuck Nelda, I thought. "F on the paper—F-minus on the paper, zero. And maybe we could turn her over to the review board for counseling or whatever?" A weasely question: half of me still wanted to back out from doing anything.

Dr. Gaines said, "That's the easiest way."

Outside, crossing the plaza in front of the Main Building as I headed back to my office, I spotted Emily—rumpled, blousy—also heading for the UGL. I hadn't read her damn chapter yet, and I knew she'd ask about it. She'd probably bitch about the damn electric bill, too, and I didn't have $20 on me to pay her off.

I turned and ducked into the side entrance of the Main Building, went down a long hall past the Bursar's Office and an information kiosk, then out the back. There was a little courtyard there with vending machines and tables—and then coming across the courtyard toward me I saw Nelda Krueger. I stopped.

"Dr. Holt!" Nelda was all grinning and cheerful. "Did you get my email?"

"Yeah," I said. In my hand was the folder with all the information on her plagiarism case.

"I'm so embarrassed! After I got your email I wondered what could be wrong, so I went and looked and saw that I sent you the wrong paper!"

"Yeah, it's a total mess," I said. I stepped back out of the way so that we wouldn't block the door. Nelda took a step toward me. I could smell her breath mints. Her shirt was open at the neck and I could see a freckle or two, and a little gold heart on a gold chain. "The situation's a total mess."

"But I'm okay, right?"

"Well," I said. "The CSP said 77% of your essay was plagiarized."

"Jeeze!"

"So I had to go show it to my boss."

"But I sent you the right paper today—that first one was a mistake."

"And I believe you," I said. I wanted to believe her, at least. Yeah. I took a deep breath, looked at her. Looked her in the eye. "I totally believe you." I remembered the soft-looking inside of her thigh on that first day of class, those tight yellow shorts—it seemed like yesterday, staring unprofessionally at a pretty girl on a hot summer afternoon. The pretty girl standing here in front of me.

"Listen," I suddenly said, "we should probably get together at some point and talk about this, you know?"

> From: Nelda Krueger
> To: Thomas Holt, PhD
> Subject: just now
>
> Hey I forgot to tell you just now that I can't come to class on Friday I'm going home for the weekend but if you want to talk to me about the paper or whatever we could maybe get together next week?
>
> Nelli ;)

They hated me, my officemates, Spanish instructors Jennifer and Marco. Jennifer was from Baltimore and Marco from Buenos Aires, and on those unhappy days when we were all in the dungeon at the same time, they would whisper to each other in soft Spanish, whisper and giggle. I had two years of Spanish as an undergraduate, and of course lived in a city that was at least 40% or so Spanish-speaking, and I could barely understand a word they were saying—I could only pick up an occasional word or phrase, like "pinche cabron" or "imbécil chingado." Imbécil chingado, and I knew they were talking about me.

Jennifer and Marco were sitting at their desks when I came back from talking with Dr. Gaines—and Nelda.

"Some woman was here to see you," Marco said. "She left a note."

"Some woman?" I asked. On my desk was a note from Emily.

> *Where are you? I thought you had office hours!*
>
> *Em!*

"Oh," I said.

"I told her you were teaching," Marco said. "You're not teaching?"

"I was in a meeting," I said. "Now I have office hours. Mis horarios de oficina."

Marco and Jennifer burst out laughing.

"What?" I asked. "What's wrong?"

"I'm sorry," Jennifer said. "But you sound like a little kid."

"Un chico tonto," Marco said.

"Oh," I said. I sat down at my desk, which faced away from Marco and Jennifer and was wedged up against a sewer pipe. Our cubicle was right beneath the first floor restrooms in the library, and whenever someone flushed a toilet, water surged and gurgled down the pipe and drowned out whatever anyone was trying to say. I sat there staring at some green ooze that was puddling at the base of the pipe: it was bigger than it had been the day before. The janitor hadn't been in to mop.

"Office hours," Jennifer said. "Horas de oficina. Say it."

"I'd better not," I said.

"C'mon," Jennifer said. "Try."

I swiveled around in my chair and gave it my best shot. "Los horas de oficina."

Jennifer and Marco laughed at me again.

"Horas," Jennifer said. "Horas de oficina."

"Puro burro," Marco said to her.

"Just keep working at it," Jennifer said.

I turned back to my desk. Dr. Gaines had given me some paperwork on Nelda's—case. Her academic integrity case. Her lack of academic integrity case. I thought of Nelda: fine brown hair, brown eyes, breath mints, the warm inside of her thigh. A stolen goddamn movie review from Texas Monthly. What an idiot! She really thought she was going to get away with that. Of course, I was an idiot, too—I had to go and tell her that I totally believed her—yeah, that I totally fucking believed her! I really *was* a dumbass.

"Hey," Marco said.

I ignored him.

"Hey!"

They just wanted to make fun of me.

"Dr. Holt?"

I turned around. A student was standing there. Travis something. From the same class as Nelda. Glancing at Jennifer and grinning. Grinning about what?

"You have a student," Marco said.

I said, "Sí."

"Hey, you got a word right!" Marco said. "Very good!"

"Sí," Jennifer said. She was correcting my pronunciation. "Try it again. Sí."

Someone upstairs flushed a toilet and a surge of water gurgled down the pipe.

"Let's go out on the patio," I said to Travis. Even if I had gotten along with Marco and Jennifer, there wasn't enough room in the cubicle for four people. There wasn't enough room for three people.

Travis followed me out through the maze of cubes, across a hallway and out into a little patio that was almost hidden between the library and the student union. We sat down at a table, under a sagging sun-stained umbrella.

"So, what've you got for me?" I asked.

"I just wanted you to look over my paper."

Travis was one of these suburban white kids who discover Hunter Thompson or Jack Kerouac and go suddenly crazy. I had them every semester, impressionable kids who read crazy books and take the worst possible messages from them, coming up with cornball cockamamie existentialist philosophies and allegedly gonzo ways of looking at the world. Travis's papers were full of never-ending endless continuous sentences marked with dashes and ellipses and Tom Wolfe-inspired running full colons and weird hyperbolic statements—most of which, really, I found kind of stupid. But if his writing was derivative, at least none of it was stolen.

Travis passed me his paper. The prompt for this assignment was to write an argumentative essay taking a stand on a problem facing the city of Austin. Travis was writing about the city's new animal shelter.

> Dogs! Cats! Weasels! Mar-fucking-supials!
> All barking howling jabbering and I can hear
> them if I open my window though I won't
> because it is cold out, and also if I opened
> the window the hounds I share my decrepit
> bungalow with would run off and commit
> suicide in front of a bus, or kill someone…
> or end up in the shelter with the other sad
> suicidal and lonesome dogs, cats, etc. But:
> if I did dare to open my window, I could
> hear them—the animals…the beasts::::evil
> creatures that would rip my heart out if they
> had a chance…drink my blood…humorless
> homeless creatures for a reason—they hate
> us::::With good reason!....

I thought of the animals now under my care—Ben, Fred. I hoped they didn't hate me. I bet they didn't. I sat staring at Travis's paper, at the stupid words, not reading them, suddenly happy about getting away from fucking people and going out to feed Ben and Fred.

Care and Feeding Instructions for Ben and Fred:

Hi, Tom—

Here are just a few thoughts on the needs of Fred and Ben:

1. Litter boxes. Using the slotted spoon provided, you will remove solid feces and clots of urine-soaked litter material from the litter box daily. Removed items should be placed into one of the white vinyl bags, then taken to the trash. To reduce the chances of contamination (i.e. ringworm and other parasites), please use the ventilation mask and rubber gloves provided. The ventilation masks are disposable and should be placed in the white vinyl bags with the feces and urine-clots. The slotted spoon and the rubber gloves should be washed with anti-bacterial soap following each use.

2. Cleanliness. Prior to every feeding, you will need to wash out the food bowls of the cats. The kitties will refuse to eat from a dirty bowl, and you really can't expect them to! Ben, especially, has a sensitive digestive system, and he may become ill if forced to eat from a dirty bowl. Wash the bowls using the anti-bacterial soap I have provided (it's on the counter next to the kitchen sink) and dry them thoroughly using a paper towel. Use each paper towel only once, and dispose of the paper towel by placing it in the trash. (Do not, of course, flush the paper towel down the toilet!)

3. Morning feeding. Each kitty should be fed one bowl of dry food each morning.

    3.1.1. Fred's (clean) bowl should contain a mixture comprised of 1/3 Platinum Puss Beef Bonanza, and 2/3 Platinum Puss Panther Mix. The proportions do not have to be exact, but pretty close to exact. Use a clean spoon, which

I have provided, to stir the mixture. Fred can tell when the mixture has not been stirred, and will refuse to eat.

3.1.2. Ben's bowl (again, clean) should contain a mixture of 1/6 Panther Mix, 1/6 Beef Bonanza, 1/6 Feline Feast Seafood Blend, 1/6 Feline Feast Black Angus Nuggets, and 1/3 Feline Feast Mature Cat Formula. Ben prefers his food layered in order (Panther Mix, Beef Bonanza, Seafood Blend, Black Angus Nuggets, Mature Cat Formula). As stated previously, Ben has a very sensitive digestive system. Though he has most of his problems in the evening, you should observe him closely at all feeding times....

4. Health. In case of illness or injury on the part of either Ben or Fred, I have left you two books on feline first aid. While I do not ask that you memorize these texts, I would like you to familiarize yourself with their contents, particularly the section on performing the feline "Heimlich Maneuver." Knowledge of the feline "Heimlich Maneuver" could be invaluable when coping with Ben's digestive tract. Of course, in case of serious, sustained vomiting, or any other medical emergency, please call our vets. The numbers are affixed here to the refrigerator door, next to these instructions.....

More to come—I'll email you!

All Best—

Camille

.

From: Nelda Krueger
To: Thomas Holt, PhD
Subject: Tuesday?

Hey I'm sorry but the only time I can see you is Tuesday afternoon will that work? Call me if you want.

Nelli ;)

In the mornings I drove out to Dr. Braddock's house—no problems getting lost once I knew where to turn—and fed the cats and then did whatever I had to do that day—grading, mostly—and then I would drive back out in the early evening for the second feeding. Ben and Fred ate all their food and seemed happy—friendly, even, once they got used to me. I ventured down the stairs twice, on the first and second days, to check on the litter boxes: I found turds and clotted clumps of cat piss. The boxes stank a little, but not too much. I sprayed around some lemon air freshener and left them. I thought, What's the point of cleaning out the boxes every damn day?

On the fifth day, Tuesday, I took Nelda along. She lived west of campus in a condominium her father had bought for her, and she was waiting outside on the steps when I drove up.

"So," she said, "we're going to go feed a cat or something? I thought we were going to talk about my paper." She snapped gum and pushed her light brown hair away from her face.

"Well," I said, "I'm doing a favor for a professor—another professor." I glanced over at her and felt pitiful—and I was pitiful: I felt compelled to remind a 19 year-old girl that I too had a PhD. Though of course I wasn't a real professor, merely a nothing nobody debt-slave adjunct instructor. "After the cats we can maybe go play some pool or something." Then I said, "Maybe talk about your paper."

The paper. We were supposed to talk about the paper.

I didn't want to talk about her stupid stolen paper.

"I like going out in the afternoons," Nelda said. I don't think she really wanted to talk about the paper, either. "Makes me feel like I'm getting away with something."

We went out Lake Austin Boulevard and crossed the river on the low bridge, then west up into the hills. The sky was clear but the sunlight was weak and wintry.

"I've been out here before," Nelda said. "I mean, I think. We came out to a party out here somewhere once. Of course we got lost."

"Getting lost can be fun."

"Oh, I know—especially if you get lost with someone you want to get lost with." Nelda smiled at me with her mouth open, small white teeth glistening and hard.

At the house I held the gate open for Nelda and we walked up the gravel path to the door. When I stuck my key in the lock Nelda put her hand on my arm to stop me.

"Aren't you going to knock first?" she asked.

"No—"

"Maybe somebody came home early—maybe there's somebody in there asleep."

"Just some cats in there asleep." I went ahead and opened the door. As always, Dr. Braddock's house had that other people's house smell—not unpleasant at all, but different. A clean smell, but not homey.

I turned on the light in the kitchen. Nelda said, "Nice."

I went into the living room. Fred was sitting staring out the window, and he turned and looked at us.

"Cute kitty!" Nelda said.

I found Ben sleeping behind a chair. I pointed at him, and Nelda came over and looked.

"Oh, he's old," Nelda said. "But he's cute, too."

"They're nice cats," I said. I pointed at the Chatham lithograph over the fireplace. In the dim light the gray horizontal river looked icy. I said, "That's Montana."

Nelda studied the print for a moment. Frowned. "Looks cold."

"Books," I said, pointing at the bookcases. "Photos." I actually felt very possessive toward everything, as if this nice, tasteful home was becoming mine, in a way, as I presented it to a new viewer. Though I suddenly realized that I could never take a girl like Nelda—or any woman at all—over to my little apartment off Burnet Road—how shabby all my possessions would look.

Shit, how shabby all my possessions were.

Ben got up and stretched and came over and rubbed against my legs.

Nelda asked, "What's upstairs?"

I shrugged. "I guess her bedroom, her office."

"You guess! You haven't been up there?"

"Uh, no," I said. "I'm not much of a snoop."

"Let's go look!" Nelda started up the stairs.

"Nelda—"

She didn't say anything, she just disappeared down the hallway at the top of the stairs. After a moment I followed, Fred and Ben at my heels. I found her in the first room on the right—a large dark bedroom. Black comforter on the bed, big new-looking TV on a rolling cart. Nelda was looking at some framed photographs on the bed's nightstand.

"Who's this with her?" Nelda asked. She held up a photo of Dr. Braddock and a woman who was maybe in her twenties. Dr. Braddock looked younger. A mountain range rose up behind the two of them—the Tetons, maybe. "Her daughter? Sister? Niece?"

"Don't know," I said.

"Is she married?"

"Don't know," I said again. I don't ask questions, not even when questions are appropriate, like in a class, and I'm not a snoop.

"You don't know!" Nelda looked at me with her open-mouthed smile, like I was making a big joke. "How come you don't know?"

"Because I don't," I said. I thought back to when I was in her office and she checked her email. There had been rings on her fingers, but no wedding ring that I could remember. I said, "I don't think she's married now."

"Well, obviously she's not married *now*," Nelda said. "Where's her husband's stuff? Where's her kids? All she's got is these cats."

Fred and Ben were sitting in the doorway watching us.

"You're sure not very curious."

"I should go feed the cats," I said.

Nelda opened a dresser drawer and started going through Dr. Braddock's underwear.

"Come on," I said.

"Ha!" Nelda pulled out a black velvet pouch closed with a drawstring. It was a foot or so long, and seemed heavy. Nelda grinned at me. "Open it," she said. "I'm afraid to look."

"Put it back."

"You're no fun," she said. She dropped the pouch back into the drawer.

Across the hall, I saw another room: Dr. Braddock's office. I went in. It was a room almost bigger than my entire apartment, wide and airy and neat, with a desk at the windwo facing the door, a computer and printer on a side desk, and more shelves with books. Photographs covered the walls, pictures of dust storms and desiccated dead cattle, and on a table by the door was neat stack of manuscript pages. I looked at the title page: *No Water this Year: Literatures of Memory and Drought in the American Southwest*. Dr. Braddock's new book, the one she'd just sent off to Oklahoma University Press.

Nelda came in and looked around. "This whole place is really sad, you know? I bet she doesn't have a friend in the world. She's just an old lady with cats."

"She's not that old," I said. I didn't point out that Dr. Braddock was better off than I was, at least— that with two books and a nice house, and a pair of cats, and an almost tenured-status, she was probably better off than I would ever be. She didn't need friends.

I turned and went back down to the kitchen. The cats raced ahead of me—hungry, I guess, since it was now early afternoon and their usual feeding time was in the mornings. Nelda tagged along and watched me rotate the bowls from the evening feeding to the morning, then measure out the portions of feed for each cat.

"That's a lot of work," Nelda said.

"Yeah, no shit."

"Are they really that fussy?"

"Dr. Braddock says they are."

"Maybe while she's gone you can train them to be not so

fussy."

"I'm not that good a teacher," I said. Nelda didn't say anything. I guess she agreed with me. We watched the cats eat. Ben seemed to enjoy his food. After awhile, I said, "The litter boxes are down here."

I led the way down to the utility room. Halfway down I could smell the litter boxes.

Nelda asked, "You haven't been down here much, huh?"

"Damn," I said. The boxes had gotten gross almost overnight—apparently some strange tipping point of cat shit stench had been reached. I turned to say something and saw Nelda going back up the stairs.

"Where're you going?"

"I didn't say I'd help you!" she called from the kitchen.

Ben was sitting at the top of the stairs washing his face. Then he stared at me.

Oh, well. This was what I had signed up for. What I agreed to do. I looked around the room. Doorway to the wash room, doorway leading outside. Bookcase with never-opened textbooks. The cat box supplies on an uncluttered workbench: disposable masks, lemon-scented air freshener, slotted spoon, trash bags, big white plastic bin of litter.

Nelda stuck her head around the corner. "Are you okay?"

"I'm trying not to breath." I fastened one of the masks around my head and picked up the slotted spoon. Both boxes were full to the brim with shit. How could the cats do so much? I thought of all the fancy layered meals I had been feeding them. All for a bunch of shit. I scooped up a rough clot of pee and shit from Fred's box and tried to slide it into a trash bag. But the bag wasn't fully open and the clot came flopping out onto the floor, where it broke apart.

"Shit!"

Everything stank. I stepped forward to try to scrape up the big pieces, but I stepped onto the edge of Ben's litter box and the whole damn thing tipped up and over—shit shooting out across the floor and my sneakers.

"God damn it!"

"What?" Nelda was safe upstairs. "Are you okay?"

I looked up. Both cats were at the top of the stairs now looking down at me.

"I need a broom," I said.

"What?"

I pulled the mask away from my face. "I'm looking for a fucking broom!"

After a pause, Nelda said, "You don't have to curse at me."

"Yeah, fuck you, too," I said quietly. I don't think she heard me: she was up there in the hygienic safety of the kitchen. I kicked the overturned box and it slid across the floor spewing cat shit. I said, "Fuck."

Ben came down the steps. He paused and looked at me, then came the rest of the way.

"This is all your fault," I said to him. "So why don't you clean it up?" Ben didn't answer.

There was a broom and a metal dustpan in the corner. I swept the floor and managed to get the shit into the trash bag without spilling anything more. Fred came down the stairs and sat next to Ben.

Nelda called, "What's taking so long?"

I pulled the mask away. "You want to come down and help me?"

No answer.

I went ahead and totally emptied both boxes and refilled them. The cat shit and piss filled two plastic trash bags. I lugged them up the stairs, leaving the cats behind me piddling in the clean boxes.

In the kitchen Nelda was drinking a glass of water, leaning against the counter. She shook her hair away from her face and smiled at me.

"That took a long time."

I didn't say anything and went on out into the garage. I put the bags of cat shit into a big green trash bin.

Nelda stood in the doorway. "This is really a lot of work she has you doing."

"Yeah?"

"So, how much is she paying you?"

I didn't say anything for a moment. How stupid I suddenly felt! Nelda stood in the doorway, bright and cheerful, smiling at me.

I shrugged. "Nothing, I guess. It's a favor."

"Wow." Nelda stood there smiling at me with her mouth open.

From: Thomas Holt, PhD
To: Nelda Krueger
Subject: Today

Hi, Nelli—

I had a fun time today. Let's do it again!

Tom

.

From: Nelda Krueger
To: Thomas Holt, PhD
Subject: re: Today

It was great, how about Friday? We could go look at Christmas lights. I LOVE Christmas lights!!!

Nelli :]

Every day I fed the cats—mixed their damn food perfectly, watered Dr. Braddock's few plants, picked up her mail, took out the trash and brought the empty trashcan back inside. I even stayed current on the litter boxes: I cleaned them daily, just like she asked me to do. I got used to it, really, driving all the way out there and back twice a day. In the evenings after I fed the cats I hung around an hour and a half, two hours, grading papers and waiting to see if Ben would vomit. A couple of times he did. Once I found the vomit a bit late and

Fred was already eating it. I cleaned the vomit up with the provided solvents and paper towels.

I was used to it. Sort of. Only sort of because I kept thinking how Dr. Braddock never said anything about compensation. All she ever said was "favor." And I agreed to do her the favor—of course. I just assumed or hoped she'd take care of me. But maybe she just meant *favor*.

I broke the numbers down. Dr. Braddock's house was just over nine miles from my apartment. Call it nine. Out and back, twice a day: that's 36 miles a day. At 50.5 cents a mile...that's $18.18 a day for transportation. For 11 days, that's $199.98.

Gasoline. My beat-up Chevy Malibu got about 15 miles a gallon on a good day. Total mileage out and back over 11 days: 396. Which is 26.4 gallons of gas at, say, $3.60 a gallon...$95.04....

Time! I figured I ought to at least get $20 an hour for feeding the cats. It took me an hour and a half in the mornings (including drive-time) and two and a half in the evenings. Four hours per day: $80. Eleven days—$880.

Added up, the numbers were appalling:

Mileage	199.98
Gasoline	95.04
Time	880.00
Total	1175.02

Holy shit!

I wrote the figures on a file card, then folded it up and put it in my billfold to remind me of my foolishness, my stupidity, my lack of a backbone—my inability to say No. The next day, when I went downstairs to clean the litter boxes, I came back up the stairs with a couple of those unopened, never-read rhetoric texts—*Everything's An Argument* and the sixth edition of *The Bedford Handbook*. Sold them that afternoon for $35. The way I looked at it, Dr. Braddock still owed me about $1150.

> From: Emily Caldwell
> To: Thomas Holt, PhD
> Subject: my chapter
>
> Hey, have you even read the chapter yet? I need to get revisions off to my chair before xmas. Let me know. Also the electric bill.
>
> Emily!!!!

The grading never stopped. Papers kept coming and coming—a blizzard of grading. A hurricane, an avalanche, a tsunami, an earthquake—a dirigible explosion, a plane crash, a train wreck, a terrorist attack. A disaster of grading. I took my work over to Dr. Braddock's in the evening, to try and get some work done while I watched the cats. The cats helped a little: Ben usually slept curled up next to me while Fred would perch in a chair, dozing, opening his eyes occasionally to see if I was still there. After a while—bored silly with bad student papers—I tossed aside the grading and picked up Emily's dissertation chapter.

"Emerson reverts to his familiar topoi in 'The Fate of the Republic,'" Emily began, "topoi that had him slowly, staggeringly, come to accept Lincoln's plan for emancipation as a wartime act."

The first sight of the word topoi made me sleepy—as sleepy as Fred or even Ben. I didn't have the heart—or the brainpower—to read any more.

Poor Emily. I always remembered that Transcendentalism Seminar—one of the last classes we'd had in grad school. She was, as always, tense and nervous and grumpy, and she rebelled against the reading. All of it. She just didn't want to do it. Emerson, Parker, Thoreau, Douglass, Whitman, all those guys. They turned her off. Even Margaret Fuller. They all made her mad. When it came time for her to give a presentation to the class, she did miserably, all red-faced and stuttering. At home that night she cried, mad at herself for doing so poorly, mad about not preparing enough for her talk, mad about having acted stupid in front of the professor and the other students. Most of all she was angry at the Transcendentalists: they were boring, they had nothing to say to the 21st century, they did not inspire her. Yet her dissertation topic—rhetorical intersections of feminists and abolitionists, or something like that—dealt almost entirely with the work of the Transcendentalists. She was stuck with them.

I looked at the chapter again. Topoi. I couldn't stand it. What the hell. I'd just lie to Emily, tell her I'd read the damn thing, tell her what a remarkable achievement it was, or whatever. Or something. Even if she knew I was lying to her, what could she say?

I tossed the chapter to the table, but it slid off a pile of ungraded essays and fell to the floor with a soft plop—soft, but the cats woke up and stared at me.

"Don't worry, kitties," I said. "Go back to sleep." I rubbed Ben's neck and he began to purr.

Of course, Emily would know I was lying—she always knew. But, really, what could she do about it? She couldn't kick me out of the house again. She might demand the rest of the electric money, but unless I stole a lot more of Dr. Braddock's old rhetoric texts, I wouldn't have anything to pay her. And even if she knew in her heart—her stony heart, small and hard as it was, her tiny coprolith of a heart—that I was lying, how could she actually prove it? Give me a quiz?

Ben rolled over on his back, still purring softly.

"What would Emerson do?" I asked Ben.

Ben opened one eye and looked at me and didn't say anything.

From: Camille Braddock
To: Thomas Holt, PhD
Subject: Ben and Fred

Hi, Tom—

California is fun, but I miss those boys a lot! I hope you're giving them plenty of hugs!

All Best,
Camille

Friday evening I took Nelda along for the late feeding. It was a dark, chilly, rainy night. Nelda wanted to go driving around and look at Christmas lights before she headed back to Dallas for the holidays. I didn't really want to do that—more gas wasted, I thought, more money spent—but in the end, of course, I said sure. Why not? I couldn't say No—not to Dr. Braddock, not to a 19 year-old girl. Still, several of the houses on Arbor Ridge were lit up, and they did look nice: one of the houses was all outlined in blue, with its trees wrapped in white, shining like ghosts. They made Nelda happy. Once we got inside Dr. Braddock's house I felt a little Christmas-y and warm, too, and so I brought out a bottle of Dr. Braddock's good Haitian rum and poured us each a glass.

"To us," I said.

Nelda took a sip and winced. "Whew! That's strong."

"Barbancourt," I said. "This is good."

Nelda looked doubtfully at her glass and went back to the living room. I sat down next to her on the couch.

"Don't worry," I said. "I'll get the cats fed and then we can go drive around and have some fun."

"It's fine here," Nelda said. "It's safe."

Safe. What did that mean? Safe. Nelda took another sip and winced again. There were some photography books on the coffee table in front of us. One was Mark Klett's re-photography series on San Francisco, re-shooting scenes of the 1906 earthquake a hundred years later.

I asked, "Have you seen this?" I flipped through the book: images of disaster and regeneration. Nelda wasn't impressed. I put the book back on the table.

"So, tell me something," she said.

"What?"

"I don't know. Something. Anything."

The big white couch was soft and sort of saggy in the middle, and it pulled us together. I put my hand on her thigh, that thigh I'd been thinking about for four months, and I felt her leg warm through the soft worn denim of her jeans. I moved my hand up her leg. I'd been thinking about that, too.

"What sort of things do you want me to tell you?" I asked.

Nelda shook her head, tilted a little toward me, and I touched her cheek, kissed her, kissed her, and soon we were grappling on the couch, clothes coming off, gasping at times, and Nelda slipped onto me, astride me, and I could see the fading tan lines on her chest and hips.

When I looked up the cats were staring at us. Ben had his ears cocked back.

I said, "The cats were watching us."

Nelda took her head off my shoulder and turned to look at the cats. "That's creepy," she said.

"Dogs get all excited when they watch people fuck."

"I know." Nelda pulled off me and fell back onto the couch. Her panties were still dangling from her right ankle and she pulled them off and held them over her belly. She looked over at me and giggled.

"I guess I should go feed the cats," I said.

"You like those cats."

"Like you better." My boxers were on the floor and I stumbled a bit trying to put them on. Nelda smiled at me. I said, "Come on, cats."

Fred and Ben followed me into the kitchen and watched as I mixed their food. In the living room I heard the TV go on, then off. I sat Fred's black Goth bowl down, then Ben's red bowl. Ben didn't even sniff at Fred's bowl when I put it down—it was like he had faith that I would be giving him his food, mixed just the way he wanted it.

"You really like this rum?" Nelda called.

"Sure," I said. "Want some more?"

Nelda came into the kitchen, soft blue panties on now and her bra, white socks on her feet. I brought out the rum, filled her glass, kissed her on the neck. She looked at the cats eating. Suddenly Ben stepped back and began to hack—*kha! kha!*—and he vomited on the kitchen floor.

"Damn," I said. "That was pretty quick. Usually he waits awhile."

Fred left his black bowl and nosed around Ben's vomit. He began to lick at it. Ben wandered off.

"Gross," Nelda said. She followed Ben back to the living room.

I got out some paper towels and began wiping at the floor. I patted Fred on the shoulder, and he was purring, happy with the vomit. I pushed him aside and cleaned the floor. From the front room I heard the sliding door to the deck open.

I took the wet paper towels out to the garage and put them in the trash bin. When I came back, Fred was still eating, back at his bowl now.

I said, "Where's Ben?"

Fred didn't say anything. He didn't even look up.

"Ben!" I called. "Come finish your din-din!"

I went to the living room. The blinds were open—the door was, too. I went out onto the deck and Nelda was standing there in her bra and panties, leaning over the railing. Dark trees stretched out before us, but everything else was lost in mist and drizzle.

"Aren't you cold?" I asked. I ran my hand down her back and she leaned into me.

"I like it cold."

"You're pretty hot." I put my arm around her. "Where's Ben?"

"He was out here a minute ago. I think he hopped down or something."

"Hopped down?"

"Jumped," Nelda said. "I think he jumped down there somewhere." She pointed out into the darkness.

"The fuck!" I bent over the railing and looked down.

"That's ten feet!"

"He's a cat—cats jump."

"He's an old cat! Jesus Christ!" I stared at Nelda. "How could you let him jump off the deck?"

Nelda said, "You're the one who's supposed to watch the cats."

"Yeah, but you're the one who left the door open." I took a deep breath. I tried not to be too pissed. But still. "You don't let cats jump off a cliff."

Nelda just stared at me with her mouth open. Not smiling open, either. Fuck her. I stuck my head back inside and reached around for the deck lights.

"Don't turn the lights on," Nelda said.

"We have to see the cat, dumbass."

"I'm half-naked!"

"Well, get some fucking clothes on and help me find Ben."

Nelda ducked inside and started looking around for her clothes. There was a big light in the corner that illuminated the deck: two chairs, an iron table, a dead begonia. Nelda's rum glass was on the railing. No sign of Ben. Two big lights on the corner of the deck lit up the strip of grass between the house and the trees. No sign of Ben.

I went back inside and began dressing. Nelda had her clothes on and was sitting in one of the chairs.

"Let's go find Ben," I said.

"Go find him yourself."

"Nelda," I said. "Listen—this is a fucking crisis, okay? You have to help me find that cat."

"It's *your* job." Nelda crossed her arms and stared at the floor. She used to stare at the floor a lot in class, too, when she didn't want to speak.

"You're the one who let him out," I said. "Help me."

Nelda stared at the floor and didn't say anything. God damn students who stare at the floor and never say anything.

"Oh, well," I said. "Fuck you."

I went down the stairs—it was time to change the damn goddamn litter boxes again—and I opened the sliding glass door and went outside. The narrow strip of grass was wet: the all-day drizzle was turning into a steady rain. Wherever Ben was, he was getting wet. I took a step and looked up. The deck was ten feet off the ground, easy. How the fuck did Ben jump all that way? Why?

Suddenly Nelda's head appeared at the railing. "What's the address out here?" she asked. "I'm calling a cab."

"Oh, don't call a cab," I said.

"Fuck...*you*." Nelda's voice sounded funny: I don't know if she was mocking me or insulting me.

"No," I said. "Fuck you!"

Nelda said, "Dr. Holt, sometimes you are such a little bitch." She disappeared from the railing and went back inside.

"Hey—shut the fucking door so Fred doesn't get out!"

After a moment the door slid shut and the blinds closed. At least Nelda didn't turn out the deck lights on me.

I looked into the dark trees. "Ben!" I called. "Beeenn..." my voice trailing off into the damp air. "Here, Kitty! Here, Ben!"

No answer. Just the soft sound of the rain. I stepped toward the tree line. I hadn't spent much time looking out the windows, but I knew the land dropped steeply away— very steeply in places, not quite a cliff, exactly, but something close to. Down at the bottom, next to the lake, there was a road and some houses. I didn't want to slip and go tumbling down the slope and bang through someone's roof.

"Ben! Ben-Ben!"

I stepped into the trees. They were mostly cedars, I think—I only study nature writers, I don't study nature, and so I know next to nothing about trees. All I could really tell was that the branches of the trees were very low and tangled, and, of course, wet. I had to stoop to move under them. Just down the hill from the house I found a trail paralleling the tree line. Made by deer, I guess. Hell, I had no idea what was out there—cat-eating coyotes, cat-killing cultists. I didn't even know if Ben was even down here. Maybe he'd gone back around to the other side of the house. I had no idea.

I slipped and slid onto my butt. No grass under the trees, no soft leaves, just hard wet limestone and sharp sticks. Then I put my hand on a goddamn cactus as I got up.

"Fuck!" I yelled. "Ben! Where are you?"

The cat didn't answer. The rain started coming down harder. I scuttled along the trail, away from Dr. Braddock's house, then passed the house of her neighbor. I ducked, crawled, scooted, all the time thinking what a fucking fool I was. Goddamn cats. Goddamn Nelda. Goddamn Dr. Braddock. Why me? Huh? Tell me that.

Two houses up from Dr. Braddock's, the deck lights were on, and sitting under the deck out of the rain I saw a cat. I froze—I didn't want to scare him away. Above him the blinds were open and I could see a Christmas tree inside the house. I thought—you fucking people up in there, don't you scare that cat. My cat.

"Ben?" I whispered. "Hey, kitty! Hey, Ben!"

Then I stepped into—nothing. What? Nothing. Space. I came down hard, very hard, on my right hand, and my leg caught on something. I felt around with my left hand. Something metal—a fucking metal culvert sticking out of the side of the hill to drain the street or whatever. I don't know. Water was dribbling out of it, though. My right hand really fucking hurt. My wrist. I pulled myself up on my elbow, scrambled up the culvert to the strip of grass behind the house. I sprawled out there in the rain for a moment catching my breath. When I looked up, the Christmas tree was still blinking in the window, and the cat was still sitting under the deck, looking at me. And the cat was Ben.

He didn't try to get away when I gathered him up with my good arm, and when we were back inside Dr. Braddock's house I let him drop to the cement floor. I sat back on the stairs and shut my eyes. Ben stepped into his box and squatted to take a piss or something. I just sat on the stairs holding my wrist. Broken, I was pretty sure—it really hurt. Really hurt. I heard Ben scratching around again, and when I opened my eyes he was stepping out of the box. He came over and rubbed up against my leg, purring. Poor old wet cat. Daring cat—led a dangerous life. Took chances. I reached down with my unbroken hand and rubbed his shoulder.

"Yeah, you're a good cat," I said.

Ben turned, looking up the stairs past me. He trembled, then dashed up the stairs. After a moment I got to my feet and made my own way, slowly, up the stairs.

"Nelda!" I called. "I found Ben!"

No answer. She was gone. A pile of Dr. Braddock's mail was tossed around: apparently Nelda got the address for a cab off an envelope. I found Fred sitting by the window, washing himself. My rum glass was sitting where I left it, and I went over and knocked back what was left. Then I got out my cell phone and called Nelda. She answered on the second ring.

"I found Ben!" I said.

"Good for you," she said dully.

"I am so fucking relieved," I said. I didn't want to tell her about my wrist. Not now, at least. "Listen," I said, "what're you doing tomorrow?"

"Nothing with you."

"What—?"

"You are such a fucking loser," Nelda said. "You're not even getting paid to take care of those cats."

"No," I said, "you're the fucking loser!" But I think she disconnected on me before I got the words out. Little bitch.

A quick trip to the **Emergency Room** could perhaps be in order when your wrist appears to be severely warped or distorted or deformed or malformed, or when you experience extreme or massive swelling and bruising, or partial and/ or complete numbness, or excessive unusual discoloration, or seriously curtailed dexterity in the fingers! Always be medically cautious but also avoid morbid anxiety: severe pain in the limb is not necessarily indicative of a broken wrist! **Your best bet is to remain calm.**

personal-home-healthcare.com

Well, it was broken. Severely warped and malformed indeed and my fingers were excessively discolored and my whole hand and arm looked like a giant ugly bruise, and there was no dexterity at all, none—and there was severe pain in the limb, too, of course.

Emily came through. Emily rescued me. Drove out in the rain and took me to the emergency room. She got lost four times on the dark twisty turny roads of Westlake, and she called me each time for directions, grumpy and severe but still on her way. The fifth time she called she was out in the cul-de-sac, Arbor Ridge, unsure what house I was in. I hurried outside, hurting, and found her car up the street a little bit and across. I waved at her with my good left hand and crossed over and got in her car.

"Jesus!" Emily said. "You look terrible! What happened?"

"One of the cats got out," I gasped. "Ben got out. I was trying to catch him and I fell down."

"You fell down chasing a cat," Emily said. "Jesus."

The ER wouldn't let me in unless I paid them $100 up front, which I didn't have. The fee went on Emily's MasterCard. She frowned. We sat for a long time in the crowded waiting room, Emily primly reading Len Gougeon's *Virtue's Hero: Emerson, Antislavery, and Reform*, me trying to shut out the sounds of squalling and blubbering children sick with whatever it is children get in the winter. Eventually I was called back for an x-ray and a splint, and a cursory inspection from a doctor.

"You don't appear to be drunk," the doctor said.

"No," I said.

"Most people who fall down on Friday nights are drunk."

"I was chasing a cat," I said.

The doctor didn't say anything. He gave me a Vicodin for my pain, and a Xanax for my nerves, and he wrote me a scrip for more Vicodin, and he sent me away. Emily was still there when I got out; she showed no sympathy for my pain, but she was still there, and she didn't grumble too much driving me around until we found an open pharmacy where I could fill my prescription—though she did grumble a bit about having to pay for the scrip.

Back at her apartment—our old apartment—I collapsed back limp onto her familiar, sagging couch, and tilted my head back and shut my eyes. Emily's cat, Lester, jumped up into my lap.

"You look terrible," Emily said.

I didn't want to answer. I didn't want to think about it. Of course I looked terrible. I deserved to look terrible. I kept my eyes closed and stroked Lester with my good hand. I could feel Emily standing in front of me. I could feel her frowning. She suspected me of—something. Maybe she could sense my unprofessional lusting, sense the Nelda molecules floating off my battered body. But—so what if she did? So what if she suspected me of anything? She still came out and rescued me.

"Falling down chasing a cat," Emily said. "That's the craziest thing I ever heard."

Well, I thought, you must have led a sheltered life. But I didn't say anything.

Emily moved away, toward the kitchen. I heard a cabinet door open, close.

"You shouldn't have been hanging around out there, anyway. It's not your home."

"I had to wait and see if Ben was going to vomit."

"Oh, bullshit."

I sat quietly. I didn't dare tell her about how Dr. Braddock had me studying the feline Heimlich Maneuver. Lester was in my lap, purring. I could hear Emily moving around.

"Here," she said. "Have a glass of wine."

I opened my eyes and took the glass from Emily. She sat down heavily next to me on the couch.

"You're such a big liar," Emily said. "A bad liar, too."

"I was reading your chapter tonight," I said. I sat up a little bit. I didn't want to disturb Lester.

"Yeah?" Emily squinted at me. She didn't believe me.

"I thought it was really good." I took a gulp of wine and three more Vicodin. And a fourth. I thought for a moment.

Her chapter: I had only skimmed maybe three pages. I tried to remember them. But they were forgettable. "Really good. You had me from the first topos."

"First—"

"I think you're really on to something," I said quickly. The Xanax was kicking in, and the Vicodins were close behind it. My brain was starting to levitate a bit: nice. The wine was helping, too. I didn't want to talk about this shit. I just wanted to go to bed. I tried to think. I said, "Morality is essential."

"Morality?"

"Emerson said that. Morality is essential. Go with that."

"I do," Emily said. "Sort of, I guess."

"More," I said. I took another gulp of wine. "Develop it some more. Put this—morality, whatever it is, in a political and social context. Look at the—the binaries—moral and amoral, war and peace, freedom and slavery. Men and women. North and South."

I glanced at Emily: she looked like she was about to cry.

"You're really on to something," I said again. "It's a good chapter. Your dissertation's going to knock people on their asses."

Emily still looked sad. "Yeah," she said. "Well."

"Has Dr. Corcoran seen it?" Corcoran was her dissertation chair.

"I'm going to send it to him this week. But he never answers his email—I never know what he thinks."

"I bet he'll love it," I said. I finished the wine and then awkwardly put the glass on an end table. I took Emily's hand and leaned over and kissed her cheek. Lester the cat rolled off my lap and looked up at me. I said, "It's a fucking great piece of work."

Emily looked at me levelly, eyes flat but warm. She said, "What about the Fugitive Slave Act?"

Lester scrambled up and jumped to the floor. I sank back onto my end of the couch, but I still held Emily's hand.

"My arm hurts," I said. "I can't think."

"But what about Emerson's reaction to the Fugitive Slave

Act? It's still an important part of his political development, isn't it?"

With my good hand I pulled Emily across the couch to me. She came slowly, heavily, and she rested her head on my chest.

"You stink," she said.

Of blood and rain and cat, I hoped—not of Nelda.

"I think you totally prove his rhetorical and political development," I said. I guessed she did. I didn't know. "The Fugitive Slave Act was a turning point."

"No shit." Emily sniffed a little. "You reek. We need to get you out of those clothes."

I didn't have any clothes at Emily's apartment, not any more. But Emily moved aside, and I got up and went into her bedroom and stripped out of my shirt and jeans and socks and stood shivering in my damp boxer shorts. There was a yellow and red afghan folded on the foot of the bed, and I draped it over my shoulders, a sort of flowery cape. I was cold and woozy.

Emily came in and looked at me. Woozy, but I took her hand and pulled her close, wrapping the afghan around us.

"Thanks for rescuing me," I said. I kissed her.

Emily said, "Well, I couldn't just leave you out there."

"You saved me." I sat down on the bed and pulled Emily next to me. We rolled back on the bed and Emily struggled and slipped out of her clothes—jeans down and over her hips and off, her shirt off, her bra off—and then we were beneath a comforter and Emily reached down and grabbed me and squeezed. Well. Hmm. Then she squeezed again.

"Baby, what's wrong?" she whispered.

"What?" I didn't feel much—not too much. Numb.

"You're tired." Emily pinched my dick.

"I don't know," I said. Emily was warm and soft next to me. I tried to roll away a little but Emily held on to my dick. "I don't know, maybe it's the Vicodin."

"Vicodin! I bet it's one of those little student bitches you've been fucking." Emily gave a yank—I felt that.

"Cut it out," I said.

"You asshole." Emily's mouth was inches—millimeters—from my ear. She was warm and soft and I felt like she was all around me. "Wear yourself out on some student slut and then come dragging over here—again."

"Emily—"

"Get out of here!" Emily yanked on me again.

"Well, let go of my dick," I said. "Jesus."

Emily let me loose and rolled away from me. She said, "Just go."

Hell. I sat up on the edge of the bed.

"Go!"

I got up and went back out to the living room. Just as I flopped down on the couch, Emily came to the door of the bedroom and stood there half-naked.

"You can't stay here," she said. "You're not spending the night on my couch."

"Oh, come on."

"Out," Emily said. She threw a sneaker at me, then another. Then my wet socks. Then my torn, wet jeans and my shirt. "Get out or I'll call the cops."

I stood up, wobbly, and put on my jeans.

"And I want the money for the electric bill tomorrow!"

I struggled into my shirt and then sat back down. The socks were too wet to go onto my feet but I managed to put on my sneakers. Emily was watching me, frowning, arms folded across her chest. I couldn't tie my shoes with only one hand, so I let the laces dangle. I stood up again.

"Emily," I said. "It's the pills."

"And I want money for the pills, too! And the ER!" Emily stomped over to the door and unlocked it and opened it. "And I want that money tomorrow!"

I went out and turned around to face the door. I said, "Bitch."

Emily slammed the door shut. I stood there a moment, shivering. Then the door opened and my bottle of Vicodin came sailing out. The door slammed shut again.

I picked up the pill bottle and shuffled down the stairs and around to the front of the apartment building. It was still raining, and getting colder. I pulled out my cell phone to call for a cab, but the phone wouldn't come on—the battery was dead or something. Well. Hell. There was a 7-11 a couple of blocks up the street. I could call a cab from there, I thought, and I shuffled up the street in the rain.

grademyprofessor.com report for **Thomas Holt**	Grade: :((Frowny Face!)
Student: "nelli-ut"	Course: RHE 306
Strengths Dr. Holt is a real easy grader I dont think he even reads anything I got a A in his class and I didnt expect that and he lets us do what we want	**Drawbacks** He looks at you like you were naked he drools at you hes creepy and hes not hott at all or even hot and you really really need to stay away from him

From: Camille Braddock
To: Thomas Holt, PhD
Subject: Kitties

Tom! I just got back, and I wanted to quickly thank you for the wonderful job you did caring for Fred and Ben. They seem very healthy and happy (though I think they are rather angry with me!) Please stop by my office, if you get a chance, or give me a call.

Merry Christmas!
Camille

Three nights a week I tended bar at Briscoe's, a nice restaurant located in an old house just south of the university. It's a quiet place: few people come there to hang around the bar, and those who do don't stay long, just stopping in for a drink or two before heading out on the town. Most nights I spent my time mixing drinks for the diners and putting up with the mockery of the waitresses, who saw me as an object for sport—a PhD in English and a bartender, ho-ho, ha-ha. And so I was surprised when, on a cold, drizzly night just before Christmas, Dr. Braddock came into the bar.

She was dressed in black again—sparkly eyes and shiny hair—wearing a leather jacket and another pair of expensive boots. A man was with her—her boyfriend, I guess—a big, square-headed man, dark hair going gray at the temples. He was very well-groomed.

Dr. Braddock stopped when she saw me. "Tom! I knew you worked extra jobs, but I didn't expect to see you here."

"Well, here I am," I said. I placed coasters on the bar for them.

Dr. Braddock ordered a glass of red wine, and the man a Glenlevit.

"Tom's the post-doc who took care of Fred and Ben when we were out in California," Dr. Braddock told the man. "They loved him."

"Yeah," the boyfriend said, "those are some fine cats."

I sat their drinks down and started to move away to give them some privacy, but Dr. Braddock stopped me.

"My god, Tom—what happened to your hand?"

I tapped my cast against the edge of the bar. "Fell off my bike. Pretty stupid, huh?"

"Oh, no! Does it hurt much?"

I shrugged. "Can't type very well—keeps me off the internet. Saves some time." I started to move away again, but once more Dr. Braddock stopped me.

"Tom, I'm so sorry—I don't have my checkbook with me." Dr. Braddock looked up at me, then her boyfriend.

"Don't worry, I'm taking care of this." The man paid for

the drinks and tipped me 12 dollars, which is pretty good, and again I started to move away.

"Tom," Dr. Braddock said. She wasn't letting me go. "I was wondering—I'm going out of town again next week, just for a couple of days, and I was wondering if you could—take care of the boys again." There were catches in Dr. Braddock's voice as she spoke, as if she wondered if she was perhaps this time asking too much. But she was still asking. "I mean, if it won't hurt your wrist or anything."

"Or if you've got plans for the holidays," the man said.

Down the bar one of the servers was waiting for me with a drink order, staring at me impatiently. Stacy, the snootiest waitress, and maybe the stupidest and most illiterate, a spacey, stoned, dope-dealing girl who'd had a bad time in freshman comp a couple of years ago and seemed determined to take it out on me, the asshole. Dr. Braddock was looking at me, too, and her big lug of a boyfriend was looking at me steadily from under his expensive haircut. Three people, and two of them at least wanted something from me—and none of them, probably, respected me. The void opened up again, my old friend infinity, final resting place of my integrity, my common sense, my desires. But now in opposition to the infinite came a tiny voice, a thought: You need to tell Braddock a lie! Tell her you have plans! I willed myself to acknowledge Stacy the waitress: I waved. In opposition to the void the little voice said, Lie! Lie! Lie! And if you can't lie to Braddock, just go ahead and tell her to—fuck off!

"Well," I said, after a moment. "I don't know. I guess I'm not doing anything."

I banished the little voice back to wherever it came from. Back! Who the hell needs imaginary voices in their lives? I went ahead and accepted the void. People can't escape who they are.

Dead Professors

We are still in Eden; the wall that shuts us out of
the garden is our own ignorance and folly.
—Thomas Cole

I have always liked to think that I am a careful person, that I pay attention to details, that I plan ahead for contingencies. But still I was shocked one afternoon when I swung through the department mail room and saw that the photographs of the dead professors were gone.

The dead professors: nearly a hundred years of them, eighty years of them at least, 8x10 black and white portraits of professors who had been members of our department; most of them male, of course, and fussy-looking, and prissy; some of them dull and tweedy, some with sparkles of intelligence flashing up from the past; some famous; most not. I had been in the department for about five years, and they had been gazing out at me the whole time; until they weren't. The walls of the mailroom were aged to a dull brown pumpkiny sort of color, except for the pale yellow-white rectangles where the photos had been; an ill-looking checkerboard effect.

"What happened to the dead professors?" I asked. The only other person in the room was Drucilla Hastings, a colleague—a Modernist, a Joycean. I guess I was asking her.

"What? Oh." Dru looked at the empty wall. "They took those old pictures down—I don't know, a couple of weeks ago. Maybe three weeks ago?"

And here I flattered myself that I paid attention to things. Perhaps I've been delusional all along.

"How long ago?" I asked.

"Two weeks? Three weeks? I don't know." Dru dropped a handful of flyers—memos, and advertisements for irrelevant lectures—into the recycling bin and plodded out, and I was left looking at the ugly, bare wall.

2.

The Strategic Planning Committee was meeting in a high-ceilinged room off the department office, and since it was the first time I'd attended in a long time, I took a seat at the far end of the conference table, with the window behind me, and tried to be inconspicuous. Still, when the Assistant Chair, Ralph Moore, came in, I asked him about the dead professors.

"You're the first one to ask!" he said. He seemed tickled by my question.

Ralph taught 20th Century American Lit surveys when he taught; teaching it poorly, I'd always heard; but he didn't teach much since his appointment as Assistant Chair.

"So, tell me," I said. "What happened to them?"

Ken Wytowski, a Victorian, a curly-headed little man going through a messy divorce, came in and sat at the table.

Ralph said, "Camille just asked about those old pictures we took down."

Wytowski smiled at me. "You know, you're the first person to ask about them."

3.

I didn't say anything more. There was no point in being patronized by these fools. I arranged the materials I had brought to the meeting: a clipboard with the (very slight) agenda for the meeting clipped to it, a yellow legal pad, my iPhone. Bringing a cell phone to a meeting, having it out on the table screen-up in full view, might, I suppose, be considered very rude, but my boyfriend, Clayton, was in the hospital after a heart attack, he was getting stents placed in his heart, and I was expecting a text or an email from him when he emerged from the cath lab. I checked my email: no new messages.

I looked up at Wytowski and didn't say anything, and blinked.

"Well," Wytowski said. He wanted me to react; I didn't. "Well, we took them down."

I looked at my phone again; ignored him. I was trying to come up with a kind but efficient way to break things off with Clayton—to dump him, yes, to move on—but his heart attack was perhaps complicating things.

It *was* complicating things.

Ralph said, "We're going to use the wall space to put up artwork by the children of department members."

"And children of graduate students," Wytowski said.

"It'll give everyone a greater sense of community," Ralph said.

"What?" I looked up from my phone, and spoke. "So— you're saying there's no community with the past?"

Wytowski smiled at me. He said, "You're the first person to even notice they're gone."

But I didn't notice very quickly; and I do try to pay attention; or thought I did.

4.

The meeting. The Department Chair came, and the Director of Graduate Studies, and three more professors, and a token fearful graduate student. The agenda, as I said, was slight, and somewhat silly, only three items.

The first item was the annual EEO training that all university employees had to take; grad students, too. The English Department was not in compliance: only 38% of personnel had taken the training.

"It's not good," the Chair said. "The Dean's been asking a lot of questions."

Everyone looked glum; even me, I suppose. No one liked the Dean asking a lot of questions. Or even any questions. After a little discussion, it was decided that Ralph would send out a strongly worded email on the listserve, encouraging, if not ordering, people to take the training.

The next item on the agenda was EDSAP, the English Department Strategic Assessment Project. From what I understood, this was some sort of utopian dream/fantasy/ nightmare to set a course for the department for the next thirty years. Thirty years: the next generation and a half; longer than many of us would be alive, probably. Wytowski had been chair of the EDSAP subcommittee and was very pleased with his work.

"It's always dangerous to—uh, anticipate—changes in technology and demographics," Wytowski said, "but I think you'll all be very—you know, excited—about the revolution we envision for the department."

I looked at my phone. An email from a student; I didn't open it. I wanted to, though: Wytowski was an ass, and EDSAP was boring and stupid.

"...the mission statement for the university, of course, says that we should be a university of the first class—and, uh, what we're trying to do is best determine *how* the department can best—uh, *participate*—in this ongoing quest for excellence— while *simultaneously* disrupting the status—"

My phone vibrated: a signal that a text had arrived. I looked down and saw that it was from Clayton. I opened it.

> hey baby I got a cathtr jmmed up my dick but I
> shd get out tmrrw I hope

Oh, Clayton.

5.

The third item on the agenda was a reminder that the Department's featured spring speaker would be Dr. Lonnie Sezler, a renowned academic motivational consultant. His visit was just a week away.

"You know, Oprah Winfrey did a special interview with him," Ralph said.

Elaine Ogren, a theorist of some sort, frowned. "We couldn't get a specialist? Someone who's actually active in the profession?"

"Sezler's written a monograph on film adaptations of Joyce," Ralph said. "And—"

"He's an independent scholar. He can't even get a job."

"So? He's been on Oprah—he doesn't need a job!"

"—and I think his current project is really very important. He's trying to elevate English Studies—"

"The profession," Wytowski said.

"Oh, great—"

"The profession as a whole. He fits in really well with the goals of EDSAP, and with our overall strategic plan." Ralph picked up a piece of paper and began reading. "'Dr. Sezler encourages people—academics—to achieve happiness and completeness in their work through embracing the new paradigm of change.'"

I heard somebody mumble, "What happened to the old paradigm of change?"

Ralph asked, "Did you see him with Oprah? He was talking about the pedagogy of joy, and how it works in concert with the pedagogy of change. He talked about the coming pastoral university. He was really very inspirational."

"The pastoral university," I repeated. Grumbled. It was the first thing I'd said in the meeting. No one responded.

6.

The meeting wrapped up with Ralph urging everyone to be excited about EDSAP. The Chair ordered us all to attend, and participate in, "Introducing EDSAP" workshops; which meant that I'd probably have to read the damn proposal or report or whatever Wytowski was calling it. Wytowski said he'd email us copies, and he left.

I was sort of backed into a the corner, and was the last

to leave, and I was piling together my clipboard, my legal pad, and my phone, when Ralph stuck his head back into the room and said, "Camille, I'd like to talk to you if you've got some time."

I looked at him blankly for a moment. Finally I said, "Sure."

Ralph led the way out of the conference room and around the corner to his office. It was bigger than mine, though his window only looked out into a blank courtyard, while my window offered a nice view of a magnolia tree.

"Sit down," Ralph said, and he plopped heavily down into his big, padded chair and began shuffling through papers. Without looking up, he said, "Listen, I've got some concerns about your classes, and maybe a worry or two."

I sat.

"Okay," Ralph said. He opened a folder and looked at some papers. "What one of the deals is, you've got a student in one of your classes who shouldn't be there."

I sat back. "Yeah?"

"Nelda Krueger?" Ralph asked. "She's a freshman?"

"Yeah," I said again. Nelda: she was in my "Narratives of the American West" class. A quiet girl; she was scared, or bored, or maybe she just never did the reading. At any rate, she never said much. I said, "Yeah, she's in my class."

"Right," Ralph said, "and she shouldn't be. She's only a freshman. She doesn't have the prerequisites."

"Oh." I sat there looking at Ralph. He looked back at me. Finally I said, "So?"

"Well, she's on your roster, so she's your responsibility."

I began, "Isn't that the registrar's—"

"No—she's in your class, so she's your responsibility."

I looked at him. What the hell?

"The new Roster and Registration Oversight Program? R-ROP?" Ralph pronounced it ARE-rop, sort of a growl. "How professors share responsibility with the Registrar's Office for the final roster of each class? How we put together an internal audit trail?"

"Since when?" I asked.

"Since last summer," Ralph said. "Didn't you get the memo? Didn't you take the training?"

"I guess," I said. Not. Did I even see a memo about R-ROP? If I did, I'd surely dumped it in the mailroom's recycling bin or deleted it from my inbox.

"If you didn't, you really need to take it—the Chair's really wanting us to get the training caught up, all the training. Makes us all look bad."

My phone vibrated again. Clayton talking about his dick again, probably. But I didn't look at it.

"What do you want me to do?" I asked. "Tell Nelda to drop the class?"

"It's too late in the semester for her to drop the class without a penalty," Ralph said. "So you really can't tell her to drop. We just want you to talk to her."

"Oh," I said. I got it. Talk to her and get her to drop on her own. Well.

7.

"She's only one of the deals," Ralph said. He picked up a different folder and looked into it. "The other deals—like for this class, the Narratives class, for example, it looks like you're having problems with student retention."

Retention: at first I thought he was perhaps referring to how much my students learned, or remembered; but no.

"You started out the semester with twenty-five students," Ralph said. "But now you're down to only thirteen." He paused and looked up at me.

"Well, eleven," I said. "Two of them never show up."

"At least they're still on your roster," Ralph said. "So the Department can still count them as students."

I didn't say anything; looked around his office; noticed nothing, except for a copy of Burke's *A Rhetoric of Motives* on the shelf behind him. I couldn't think of what that might mean for me. Nothing good.

"I downloaded a few of your syllabi and looked them

over," Ralph said. He pulled a copy of the Narratives syllabus out of the folder and opened it on his desk. There was nothing wrong with that syllabus; I was proud of it.

"In this class, you've assigned your students to read nine books," Ralph said. "Big books—"

"I don't think it's that much reading," I said.

"It sure looks like a lot," Ralph said. "Richard Slotkin, Ken Kesey, Rebecca Solnit, Mark Twain, Joy Harjo, Lesley Marmon Silko, Larry McMurtry, Terry Tempest Williams, Cormac McCarthy, James Welch, Patricia Limerick—"

"Challenging texts," I said. "That's what the students need."

"Two movies. *The Big Lebowski, The Searchers*." Ralph was still looking at the syllabus. Reading it aloud. I already knew what it said; after all, I wrote it, I taught it. Ralph said, "A midterm exam, a short paper, a presentation, a long paper. That's a lot of work for an undergraduate class."

"Really?" I was starting to get a little pissed. "It's not even half of what I assign my grad students."

"It's too much," Ralph said. He looked up at me, sat back. "It's just too much. And I think that's why you're losing students. You assign too much work. It's just impossible for them."

"Yeah, for the slackers," I said. My phone vibrated again and I glanced down at it: Clayton. Really. Great timing there, Clayton. I said, "I don't know—I think it's an entirely appropriate amount of work—I mean, the students who are still in the class are totally committed!"

"Well. Maybe." Ralph shrugged. "At any rate, you're losing students. The Department's losing money. And this is the sort of thing that the tenure committee pays attention to."

"Tenure? Hey, I have two books." It was only now that I realized that I was in trouble; only now that I noticed that something was very wrong. And I really do try to pay attention. The tenure committee! Holy shit. Ralph sat back in his chair, eyeing me, his gray beard all pointy and well-trimmed; pointing at me. Like a gun, like a missile, like a big hairy knob. I said, "Well, one book out, and another coming out next year."

"And we're all very impressed with that—really, it's a huge scholarly accomplishment." Ralph was trying not to sound patronizing; but failing. Badly. "But, you know, the committee looks at other things, too." He waved the syllabus. "Student evaluations. Student retention. Collegiality. Service."

"Service."

"We were really happy to see you at today's meeting," Ralph said. "I think that was—what, the first meeting you've attended in a year? Maybe over a year?"

"I've been busy," I said.

My phone vibrated again.

I looked at Ralph and nodded.

8.

On the way to Clayton's room at the hospital I ran into Ted Cook, one of his colleagues at the law firm. He was a big man, like Clayton, coming from the office in his sharp gray suit, tie loosened at the collar. He put his big hand on my shoulder.

"Camille, we're all counting on you to take care of our boy."

Then he was off, no doubt back to his downtown aerie. But I thought: take care. And: our boy. What the hell did that mean? I saw Ted wave at me as he got onto the elevator, and then I turned and went up the hall.

Clayton was in his bed, staring at the switched-off television on the wall across the room. A big man, on the heavy side, his hair was still precisely trimmed, though he was stubbly and unshaven.

After a moment he saw me. "Baby," he said, "we've got to get me out of here."

I kissed him on the forehead, then sat down next to his bed. He was hooked up to all kinds of things: there was an IV running into his right forearm, the catheter tube snaking out from under his gown, there was something clipped to his left index finger, and a mass of wires ran from his chest to one of those heart-beeping machines like you see on television.

"Tomorrow," I said. "They said you can go home tomorrow, right?"

"I guess," Clayton said. He sounded weak and depressed. He was still staring ahead glumly. "But who knows, maybe they're all a bunch of liars."

"I bet they're not." I slouched back in the chair, put my feet on a stool. I wasn't sure what I should do: I'm not a nurse, I'm an English professor; a Doctor of Philosophy, not a physician. I suppose I could have read to him. I asked, "So, what was the procedure like?"

"They gave me lots of morphine," Clayton said. "Stuck in three stents—said one artery was 90% blocked."

"Damn."

"Yeah." Clayton sighed. "I guess it went okay. They kept me doped up."

I sat up and put my hand on his forehead: cool, damp. My sad attempt at nursing. I said, "You're doped up now."

"I can't even focus to read. I think all I want to do is sleep."

I said, "Then you should sleep."

9.

Clayton, Clayton. I looked at him sleeping; wondered; worried. What was I supposed to do with him?

He loved me, I think; he said he did, often enough. I'd mumble "love you too" at the end of a phone conversation, but it made me uncomfortable. I didn't want to lie to Clayton, even if I didn't exactly love him. I liked him and admired him; maybe that wasn't enough. He was a successful and interesting man: attorney, citizen, home-owner. Lover of English professors and barmaids and small dogs. Ex-husband twice, father once. Reader of books. Drinker of scotch. Owner of a damaged heart.

I wasn't there for his heart attack. I only know what I was told: there was growing discomfort in his chest all afternoon at work. I could picture him in his office on the 19th floor, standing there in Olympian splendor, looking west out over the city, people jostling about their lives on the street far below him, the river stretching out, hills rising up on the smoggy distant horizon—my house in those hills, of course, and I wonder if he looked out and thought of me.

Probably not; probably not, at least right then. There was something wrong in his chest, the sort of something wrong that any overweight, middle-aged, over-stressed, drinking, smoking man anticipates without even acknowledging the anticipation. The heart—now. Something was wrong.

And so Clayton told his secretary that he was going out for a smoke, and he went down the hall, got into an elevator, went down 19 floors to the lobby, and stepped outside onto the plaza. Lit a cigarette. Exactly what you're supposed to do when you're a middle-aged, overweight man faced with chest pains: have a smoke, think it over.

The plaza outside Clayton's building is below street level, to shut out the sounds of the city, a little, and has a long fountain where water flows in rippling hissing sheets down a wall. It was a warm, sunny, day, breezy with a few cumulous clouds. Spring. He smoked, thought, made a decision: Time to go home.

10.

At one point in my life, back into history, back before I got a PhD in literature, I got an MFA in creative writing. I had ambitions of being a writer, a real writer, an essayist, a memoirist, not an academic writer. The main thing I got from my MFA, besides an unpublishable book, was a realization of the anxious, complicated relationship of the individual selves: the self of today and the self of the past, and how they engage in an endless game of hide and seek, a contest that neither one will ever win, since the landscape of time and memory are constantly shifting, constantly transforming one Self to the Other. We never really know who we are; or why. It took me three years to figure that out; years more to understand what it might mean.

My past self was married to a poet, a handsome, rugged guy who liked to hunt and fish and participate in other manly, unpoetic activities. One year he went off to a summer workshop and came home in love with another poet, a strange, creepy, morbid woman who he claimed understood him like no one else ever had or would.

When my Self of today told Clayton that story, a story my Self of the past thought was very sad, he laughed and laughed. He asked, "Why are you so sad? That was a good thing, you know? You escaped a trap!"

11.

On the day of his heart attack, Clayton made some excuse to his secretary, gathered up his jacket and his briefcase, and went home. He went home: way out on the southwest edge of town; not to the hospital emergency room downtown, a mere 15 or so blocks north of his office. It was late afternoon, and traffic was getting heavy—heavier, this is, after all, Austin—and he stopped and started along, listening to Lucinda Williams on his nice car sound system. At home, he let his little rat terrier, Scumbo, out to pee in the back yard. He went up to his bedroom and changed into a pair of khaki shorts and a golf shirt and sneakers. He came back downstairs and poured himself a glass of scotch; sat down, smoked a cigarette. Ignored Scumbo, who wanted to play. He was still feeling discomfort; pain, really. He told me later he knew what it was, but he just didn't want to do anything about it.

But after a while, he did. He got his car keys, got in his car, and headed for the emergency room. Backing out of the driveway, he called me.

12.

My then-husband would try to include me in his manly outings, but I didn't have the rhythm for fly casting and I was afraid of guns. He suggested bird-watching: I could watch birds while he fished and hunted. My thesis director was all for bird-watching, too: he was a nature writer, a bird writer—a bird brain, I later came to think. But I found birds to be nervous little creatures who were always hopping around or flying away, and most of them were small and brown, or small and gray, or small and brown-gray. I couldn't tell them apart. Both my husband and my thesis director thought I was obtuse and stubborn; and maybe I was. Then I discovered clouds: I could watch clouds. They moved slowly, and though they were always changing, they changed without the nervous energy of birds. I could identify the basic cloud types—cumulous, cirrus, stratus—and try to understand the subtypes. I liked clouds. I liked having my head in the clouds.

And so, on a pleasant spring evening, I was out on the deck of my townhouse with one of my cats, Fred, sitting on a metal chair, with my feet up, a glass of wine beside me, taking a few minutes to study the sky and think a bit before I went in to fix dinner.

My phone rang.

13.

Clayton said, "Well, I don't know—maybe I'm going to the emergency room."

I sat up; put my feet on the deck. "What?"

"I've got this—I don't know." Clayton sounded confused: that alone was shocking to me. How could Clayton ever be confused? "Something in my chest—I'm gonna have it checked out."

"Fuck, yes, you're going to have it checked out." I got up and started shooing Fred inside; Fred looked at me angrily. "Which hospital are you going to?"

"Southwest," he said.

"Okay," I said. Southwest wasn't far from his home. "Okay, I'm on my way."

I disconnected. Poor Clayton—poor me! I'd been sitting on the deck looking at cheerful puffy cumulous clouds, thinking, pondering, wondering how best to let things cool down between us, how to let things *end*, and all of a sudden Clayton was dying.

14.

Now, a few days later, we sat quietly in the hospital. Clayton dozed, and woke up. Voices echoed in from the tiled hospital hallway, where nurses and other mysterious people were out there were doing whatever mysterious things it was they did.

"Had a big ruckus here last night," Clayton said. "Some old lady died, and the whole family went to shit."

I said, "Aww."

"They should have left those kids at home," Clayton said. "I hate hearing kids cry."

I asked, "Has Andrea been in to see you?"

Andrea was Clayton's daughter from his first wife, 23 years old and doing clerical work at a state agency; something of a disappointment to Clayton. I hadn't met her until the heart attack.

"Maybe," Clayton said. "I've been doing a lot of sleeping."

"Poor baby."

"I think I'm hungry," Clayton said. "I wish they'd bring me something good to eat."

I shifted in the chair. "You know, you're going to have to change your diet, now. No more heavy meat, less alcohol, more vegetables."

Clayton pulled the covers up to his chin; some of the wires coming out of his chest tangled for a moment, but before I could reach to untangle them, he was able to do it himself.

"I like broccoli," he said.

I laughed, "I've never seen you eat broccoli!"

Clayton looked up at me, stared; bleary-eyed. "You're not around me twenty-four hours a day—maybe I eat broccoli all the fucking time when you're not around."

"Maybe. I doubt it."

"I'm the fucking king of broccoli-eating." Clayton shifted again, uncomfortable. I reached and squeezed his shoulder. "Listen," he said. "Tell me the truth? When I get out tomorrow? You're going to be here?"

15.

English 379N, "Narratives of the American West," had, as Ralph so helpfully pointed out, 25 students at the beginning of the semester, and now, at the end of March, swinging into the home stretch, had a mere 13. Ten of them were there when I walked into the dim little room in the basement of Calhoun Hall, all juniors and seniors, except for Nelda Krueger. As best I could understand the R-ROP report, Nelda had taken composition but not intro to literature. She was a quiet girl who seldom participated in class; if I asked a general question, to get class discussion started, she'd stare at the seminar table in front of her, or the wall across from her, or maybe the tiny grimy window up in the corner; maybe, then, of course, she was praying. Praying might have helped her grade. I couldn't understand why she'd taken the class. Still, she was there.

We were covering Albert Bierstadt, an artist I always liked teaching. The text I'd assigned talked about Bierstadt's images of empire, and Manifest Destiny, and those ideological concepts were there, of course; but I much preferred to just look at slides, look at the paintings with the students, look at them and talk about them, about those strange glowing fizzing cloudscapes and landscapes that could exist nowhere in nature but only in the imagination of the artist.

At the end of class I asked Nelda to wait up. She looked startled, but she walked slowly up to my end of the seminar table.

"So," I asked, "did you like Bierstadt?"

"The pictures? Yeah, they were pretty."

Pretty pictures. It was a start, I guess. Maybe. I remember when I was first teaching composition, in grad school, and I was only four or five years older than my students. One of my professors said, "You're so lucky, you can *relate* to them." I thought then, think now, Why? Why should I relate to them? It's their job to relate to me; and if not to me, then to the material I try to teach. And besides: I've always had difficulty relating to anyone; all the people I've ever known have always seemed at a distance, living out inexplicable and baffling lives. All I could ever do was watch.

Now Nelda Krueger stood in front of me. What was her life like? I had no idea. I never would. I pulled a copy of her R-ROP report from a folder and looked at it.

"They're telling me you don't have the prerequisites for this class," I said.

Nelda looked puzzled. She was a pretty girl with dark brown hair and eyes. She was wearing a blue knit shirt that was a little too tight for her; probably she'd gained a some weight, as first year students usually do.

After a pause, she asked, "Yeah?"

I said, "You're supposed to have composition and intro to lit for this class, and you don't have intro."

Nelda bit her lip, a strand of hair falling over her left eye.

"All you took is rhetoric and writing," I said.

"Right," she said. "I took that from, uh, Dr. Holt."

"Tom Holt?"

"Yeah, I guess."

Tom Holt, a former student of mine. A very sharp young post-doc.

"I got an A." Nelda relaxed, slumping her shoulders, resting her hand on the table. She smiled, a little.

"So I see." I looked at the transcript; my eyes fuzzed, glazed. Really, it was so much bullshit to me. R-ROP was bullshit, too. I was suddenly irked by the task they were pushing onto me. They: the English Department, the Registrar's Office, other administrators elsewhere. The deal was that Nelda was in the class. She'd made her decision, paid her money, and if she was going to fail, she'd fail. Fuck R-ROP.

Nelda asked, "What should I do?"

16.

Clayton's daughter, Andrea, was standing sulking outside his door when I got to the hospital, standing with her lips all pursed up, like she was bored or angry or sucking on a lemon. Sullen.

"He's in a really bad mood," Andrea said. "I don't even want to be around him."

I stepped into the room. Clayton was sitting on the edge of the bed, wearing a new pair of gray sweatpants and a UT t-shirt. He brightened up when he saw me.

"Camille!" he said. "They finally took the damn catheter out—did you ever have a catheter?"

"No—"

"It's no fun when they take it out. It's pretty damn rugged. Now they just have me sitting here, waiting to go—waiting and nobody's telling me how long it'll take."

"Daddy, it hasn't been that long." Andrea was standing in the doorway, still pouty-looking.

Clayton seemed nervous and anxious; depressed, too, maybe. "I'm just sick of all this—shit."

"Of course you are," I said. I patted him on the shoulder and sat on a chair next to the bed.

"We're waiting for the doctors to sign the release papers," Andrea said.

"Taking too damn long," Clayton said. "Just a bunch of motherfuckers...."

I looked at Andrea: she rolled her eyes and ducked back out of the room. I put my hand on Clayton's arm. I said, "It'll be just a little while longer."

"You don't know." Clayton gripped the side of this bed and struggled to his feet. I saw that he was unhooked from the IV.

"Clayton—"

"Fuckers want me to walk, I'll walk. I'll walk all the way home." Clayton stepped painfully toward the bathroom, bent a little at the waist, more shuffling than actually stepping; but heavily shuffling. To place the stents in his heart, the doctors had gone in through the femoral artery in his groin, slinking the stent and whatever other probes they were using up through his trunk to the blocked arteries of his heart. Now there were stitches in the entry wound, and he shuffled heavily along like a sick, old Frankenstein.

"See?" Clayton asked. "I walk fucking fine. You need to go tell the doctors."

"Maybe you should sit down," I said. I didn't want to get involved with the physicians.

"I'm walking fine." Clayton made it over to the window and stood unsteadily, holding on to the curtain.

17.

A nurse, a trim little Asian woman in beige scrubs, hurried into the room. She asked, "What are you doing walking?"

"They told me to walk."

"You need to sit and take your pill." The nurse took Clayton's arm and led him slowly, painfully, back across the room to the bed and sat him on the edge. She said, "Be still, take your pill, chill."

"This is the only good one," Clayton said to me. "The rest are all shits and morons."

"You're crazy," the nurse said. "You just need to sit and be quiet." She offered Clayton a paper cup with a pill in it, and he swallowed the pill and then slowly took a drink of water.

"That's a nice Xanax," the nurse said. "It'll calm you down."

"I don't need to be calm, I need to be home."

"They're signing your release now," the nurse said, and she bustled out.

"She's the best one," Clayton said again. "She's the one that took my catheter out."

"Well, that was a good deed!" I was trying to be cheerful; I didn't know what else to say. I'd never seen Clayton like this before; never seen him depressed or agitated, never seen him angry, even. He was a big, smart guy; kind of cocky in a lawyerly way, but never rude. He didn't even cuss very much, at least around me. And he was always in control; except now he wasn't. Now he was just sitting on the bed, hollow-eyed and sick-looking; and angry.

"The rest of 'em are a bunch a shits."

I felt helpless. "Baby, what can I do?"

"Keep me from killing those shits."

"Okay," I said. He didn't look like he had the strength to kill anyone; to do anything. I stood up and looked around the room: a couple of green backpacks sat stuffed on the other chairs, and all the flowers and plants and balloons people had brought him were arranged neatly on a wheeled table. I said, "Looks like you're all packed up and ready to go."

"Well, Jesus Christ, I've been ready for five goddamn hours!"

"Clayton," I said.

Andrea came in then with a big young man dressed in pale green scrubs. He didn't have the presence of a physician; a nurse, maybe, or an orderly. A technician?

"Motherfucker," Clayton said to him. "Asshole. Piece of shit."

Andrea said, "Daddy—"

Clayton looked at me. "This is the piece of shit that's been holding everything up."

The young man dropped some papers on the plant-covered table. "Everything's set," he said. "You can go." He left the room.

"Motherfucker," Clayton said. Surly and mean.

I looked over at Andrea. What the hell? But Andrea just moved to her father's side and took his elbow, and helped him to his feet.

18.

Scumbo, the fuzzy little gray terrier, was happy to see Clayton when we got home, but we had to put him outside: there was the danger of Scumbo hopping up on Clayton and opening the stitches on Clayton's upper thigh; a bad thing. Scumbo sat at the back door, sad, looking in hopefully at Clayton.

Clayton was calmer when we got him home: the Xanax was taking effect, presumably. He sat in his big chair with his head tilted back, staring at the ceiling. Depressed-looking.

Andrea slumped around unpacking: dirty hospital clothes to the laundry room, plants to various sunny spots. I felt useless.

I asked, "Would you like something to eat?"

"Barbecue," Clayton said. "Maybe a big steak."

"Maybe a chicken breast," I said. "Maybe half a chicken breast—with lots of broccoli."

"Fix me a drink?"

"With that Xanax? And all your other meds?" I got up and looked at some of the books on his shelves. Lots of fiction: Larry McMurtry, Cormac McCarthy—Hemingway, Oates, Roth, Morrison. Big books by James Michener. Stephen King, too, and Tony Hillerman. Richard Price. History, big popular works of American history, the Civil War, the West. Biographies of Churchill and Truman and all the Caro biographies of LBJ, and others. Lots of books: a library. I said, without looking at him. "We're going to take care of you."

Clayton snorted; but not angrily. "You're no fun."

Andrea trudged in with an armful of sheets and pillows, to make a bed on the couch. Clayton wasn't allowed to climb the stairs for a day or so, to protect his stitches. Andrea was going to stay with him, sleeping in the guest bedroom. I was going to do, apparently, nothing. I felt like an intruder; a useless intruder. I looked at the patio door, where Scumbo was looking in at us.

"Look at that little guy," Clayton said. "He loves me. He's the only one."

19.

At home I sat with my cats, sat for a long time with a glass of wine looking out at what I could see of the night sky; mostly, the big patio door reflected back the yellow lights of my living room, but the band of black at the top gave an illusion of nighttime dark-sky infinity.

"Oh, kitties," I said. "What're we going to do?"

They didn't know; probably didn't even care. Fred, the yellow tomcat, lay next to me on the couch, purring, while Ben, the older gray tabby, was curled up across the room.

They didn't know, didn't care; but they were a comfort.

Fucking Clayton. Why'd he have to have a heart attack?

There were two stacks of paper on the coffee table in front of me: the EDSAP proposal, which Wytowski had sent along as a .pdf file, forcing me to print it out myself, and a much smaller stack of term paper proposals from my Narratives class. I wasn't sure which one I wanted to read first; or last.

I reached over and picked up EDSAP: 273 pages, half a ream of paper and who knows how much toner. Wytowksi's baby, this report. I guess writing it gave him something to do after his wife left him and his girlfriend graduated.

I looked at the table of contents: chapters dealing with the last five years in the department, chapters outlining goals for the next 30 years. Thirty! I still couldn't get over that. Thirty years: it was crazy.

I looked at a random page:

> …The disinclination of undergraduates to consume and process hard-copy texts is expected to continue; this continuation suggests that the department should begin the transmission of non-text-based courses, or, in some cases, alternatively-text-based courses. Adoption of web-based courses will enable faculty to interact with more students with less demand for physical classrooms

Oh, bullshit. Administrators were always trying to force professors to teach online classes; and only online classes. Here, Wytowski illustrated their desires with pretty charts. I didn't want to look at the pretty charts. The stupid charts. I flipped through some more pages.

> …the increasing importance of Digital Humanities to the study of texts ensures that the English Department will continue to have a leading role in the future of the College of Liberal Arts.

Digital Humanities was the hot new field. Some projects, like the Walt Whitman Archives at Iowa, and the Emily Dickinson Project at Maryland, were truly great aids to scholarship. Others, like the Digital Southwest Project put together by our own department, were just wastes of time and money. Helen Thompson, whose office was just across the hall from mine, had gotten an enormous grant to do something called The Digital Southwest, and all she had to show for it was some pretty pictures of Big Bend juxtaposed with some quotes from Frank Dobie's *Tongues of the Monte*. How was that going to advance knowledge?

I looked at another page.

> …auditing and assessment are crucial to the future success of the Department. Faculty must be held accountable for the amount of knowledge and information transferred to students….

Phooey. Fuck it. Forget it. No way I was going to read 273 pages of that shit; no way I was going to really read one page of it. EDSAP hurt my brain. I tossed the report back onto the table, and the unbound pages parted and slid across the glass tabletop. Fred opened his eyes and looked at me sleepily.

I reached for the small stack of student paper proposals; eleven of them. All that was required was a paragraph or two outlining what subject they wanted to research for their term paper. Most of the time students came up with something more or less reasonable: *The Big Lebowski* as a postmodern Western, the nationalist rhetoric of William Henry Jackson's photography (a topic I often got, since it touched on some of the themes of my first book (and my dissertation), and some delusional and perhaps suck-up students thought I might like that), Mark Twain as a chronicler of the boom economy, the roles of women in the historical and modern west. Most of the proposals at least had an argument to make, even if it was an incoherent or weird one; but then I came to Nelda Krueger's proposal. Her handwritten note.

i want to write about how people moving
to the Western part of the US what people
thought about it cowboys.

Jesus, I thought. You got an A in Tom Holt's class?

20.

In the afternoon, just after my graduate seminar let out, I went down the stairs and out the front door of Parlin and onto the South Mall. A pleasant spring day: sunshine filtering down through the usual cumulous, down through the leaves of the trees, a light breeze. The campus was hot and calm in the shade of live oak trees: late afternoon, and already the students were heading off to whatever trouble they could find.

The lobby of the undergraduate library was eerily quiet, and I went down the stairs to the basement level. I had never been down there before; never needed to. A long, empty, lobby-like hallway ran down the length of the building, glassed in on the west side, facing a little sunken courtyard; across the courtyard was the student union. My boots click-clacked on the floor, and then I came to a door on my right.

Through it, a warren. That was the only way to describe it: a warren of little cubicles marked off by ill-looking beige-gray-green-brown partitions, the fabric on most of them torn, stained, and tattered. The ceiling loomed down on me—on the room—chunks broken out of the no-longer acoustic tiles with a few flickering florescent lights scattered here and there. Behind me was the brightly-lit and even almost cheerful lobby.

"Can I help you?" A dumpy, dull young woman with flat brown hair looked up at me from a desk.

"I'm looking for Tom Holt," I said. "Room 2-R?"

The woman sighed, as if she were exasperated with me. There were greasy stains on the front of her blouse. "It's back by the wall," she said. "I think."

There was no direct aisle through the warren; it was, I

guess, more like a labyrinth, twisting and turning through and past cubicles of people who sat there looking fat and depressed. People who sat there in the hell of the adjuncts.

Tom Holt was sitting at his desk, facing the wall. A slimy green pipe ran from the ceiling to the cement floor. Someone upstairs flushed a toilet, and the pipe gurgled. Two other people, a man and a woman, sat crammed into the cubicle with Tom; they looked at me silently.

"Tom?" I asked.

He swung around in his seat; cross, then stunned; then surprised. His jaw dropped. "Are—are the cats okay?"

"They're fine!" I said. I tried to sound cheerful. The other two people in the cubicle were staring at me, creepily; unsettling. I forced a smile at Tom. "I just wanted to ask you something."

"Ask me something?"

"In private." I looked at his two officemates.

"No hablo ingles," the man said.

Someone upstairs flushed a toilet again.

I said to the man, "Tengo que hablar al profesor Holt."

"We can step outside," Tom said.

"You shouldn't have to leave your office." I was staring back—glaring, maybe—at the Spanish-speaking man. The woman was smiling at me, a little, watching us; amused? But her smile made me even a bit more mad: it was Tom's office, too. Maybe the officemates should leave.

"Hablele," the man shrugged.

Someone flushed the toilet again—and again. The old pipe shuddered; groaned.

"It's better if we go outside," Tom said. He stood up but there was not enough room for him to get around me. He stood inches from my face looking—nervous, I guess. Scared. I stepped back, into another cubicle. A chubby blond woman with acne scars on her cheeks was staring at me, too.

"It's better if we go outside," Tom said again. He began leading the way out. I watched him go, stared at him, his baggy chinos all saggy in the rear. Poor Tom!

21.

Outside, on the patio, we sat at a table under an umbrella. Tom slouched back in his chair, then lurched forward and planted his elbows on the table; nervous.

"So, they really keep you guys crammed in there like that?" I asked.

"Yeah," Tom said. "It's not so—" He stopped and looked at me. Smiled a little. "No, yeah, it pretty much sucks."

"I guess." The life of an adjunct, I realized: all those sad articles I'd read about the declining professorate were sitting here right in front of me. Poor Tom. He deserved better. "How many classes are you teaching?"

"Six," Tom said. "Comp and intro, three of each."

"Six classes!" I was teaching two classes spring semester. I felt a little guilty. And six classes of comp and intro: how many students was that? How many papers did he have to grade? Poor Tom!

"You get used to it."

"Really?"

Tom shrugged; a depressed, tired shrug. "It's almost over," he said. "I got that job at Southeast Kansas State."

"Southeast Kansas," I repeated. Wherever the hell that was. Still, it had to be better than teaching six classes chained to a sewer pipe. "Good! That's tremendous!"

Tom slouched back in his chair again. "Yeah, it's tenure-track—I'll even have health insurance."

"Well—good for you!" I couldn't think of anything else to say. Southeast Kansas. Poor Tom. I pulled out my folder and opened it. "Look, I need to ask you about one of your students—one of your former students, I mean. I have her in my class—in one of my classes."

"Oh, yeah?"

"Nelda Krueger," I said. I pushed Nelda's paper proposal across the table to him. He didn't look at it; looked back at the dungeon, frowning. Pensive. I said, "She says she got an A in your class?"

"Yeah?" Tom looked at me, then past me. Even in the

dappled spring sunlight under the umbrella, I could see him blush.

I said, "You have so many students you probably don't remember...."

"No—no, I remember her...."

"See," I said, "she got into my class by accident." I paused. There was no reason to confess my failure to R-ROT Nelda out of my class; no reason to acknowledge my responsibility. "She doesn't have the prerequisites, and I have to figure out what to do with her."

Tom glanced at the proposal, then up at me.

"She says she got an A in your class," I said. "And that's on her record. But, then, yesterday she turned in that proposal to me, and—well, it's what you see."

Tom read the proposal again, all 21 unpunctuated words. He looked a long time at it.

"I remember her," Tom finally said. "She came to class, she did the work."

"But she got an A? Look at this stupid proposal!"

Tom pushed the paper back across the table to me. He said, "I don't know what happened. Maybe she was in a big hurry or something."

22.

Walking up to Parlin, and I stopped short, looking a big bronze statue just outside the door: Robert E. Lee. I stopped, and maybe noticed something. Lee: what did Lee have to do with the university? With Texas? It occurred to me that there was perhaps a connection of some sort: EDSAP, R-ROP, the adjunct dungeon, unprepared students. Lee: the Confederacy. Slavery. Treason. Was there, maybe, a connection? I had walked past that stature almost daily for almost six years, but had never really looked at it before. Robert E. Lee. Huh.

I knew of course the story about the design of the south mall: how the artist, Pompeo Coppini, had intended to create a sculpture group symbolizing the unification of North and South following the Civil War. But the statues were all south-oriented. Some of them Texas-oriented. Was that the same thing?

Robert E. Lee. In his Confederate uniform, all bearded and noble; and white. I took out my phone and clicked on the camera function. Aimed it at the Marble Man—well, the bronze Marble Man; took a photo. And other, from a slightly different angle.

There was a statue next door at Calhoun Hall, too; Albert Sidney Johnston, another Confederate general. I walked over and looked at him, also all bronzed and in his uniform. Students came in and out of the building, passing the statue without looking. He was from Texas, at least; buried in the State Cemetery. Had an Austin high school named for him.

23.
My phone tingled: a text coming in. It was from Clayton.

ur ignorng me

Not now, Clayton. I was on to something; something. I hit reply and texted back.

Yes, I am.

A few seconds later the phone rang. Clayton. I hit a red button to ignore the call; felt a little guilty.

But not *too* guilty.

24.
I circled down a little bit and walked around the Littlefield Fountain, a busy Coppini sculpture featuring a winged Victory high above water-spouting porpoises and trident-bearing nymphs wearing World War I helmets. A monument to veterans of the Great War, named for an old Confederate, George Washington Littlefield, who'd been in important figure in the early days of the university. I took two or three photos of the fountain and circled around to the east

side of the mall.

John H. Reagan was the first statue. A U.S. Congressman from Texas before the war and after the war; Postmaster General of the Confederacy during the war. He had an Austin high school named for him, too.

I looked back across the mall and up at Lee. He had an Austin elementary school named for him. Were there any buildings in Austin—heck, in Texas—named for Union generals? Grant, Sherman, Sheridan—where were they?

I took two pictures of Reagan and moved up the mall. The next statue was James T. Hogg, a Texas Governor of the progressive era. His father had been a Confederate general. Hogg was very fat, which might or might not mean something.

There were three statues at the top of the mall: George Washington, Woodrow Wilson, and Jefferson Davis. Southerners all. Washington, the first president, and Wilson, the first southerner elected president after the civil war. Davis, of course. I took pictures of Washington and Wilson and moved over to Davis.

The statue had been defaced and graffiti-ized several times in recent years, a focus of student resentment of its representation of the racist past, and the statue's pedestal was pale and white where paint had been scrubbed off. I took a photo of Davis, his head wreathed in big puffy cumulous clouds. I looked back down the mall. Memory was being performed here, of course. The memory would have been a different one in the 1920s, when Coppini cast the sculptures, but they were still in place, and 90 years later they were still remembering something; something. Even though the university tried to ignore it, this remained the bedrock of Texas: treason and slavery. It made sense now that I so seldom had a black student in my classes, that there were only a couple of thousand African American students on a campus of over fifty-thousand. From my position of privilege I'd never really considered before what a white university this was, and it *was* a white university; but the whiteness was a result of the whole history of the state. The Texas Revolution was even past beyond the Civil War honored here on the mall, but those white guys were traitors, too, traitors to Mexico, and one of the problems they had with Mexican rule was Mexico's abolition of slavery. The state couldn't get away from slavery. Tom and the other adjuncts weren't slaves, not by any means, but they were victims of the plantation-oriented economy the whole state ran on, the university, too, a top-heavy corporate oligarchy that had its roots deep in human misery.

In the limestone just below the statue's base was a large gash: a bullet's scar. I ran my finger along the gouge, soft and weathered now, and I looked up at the Texas Tower.

25.

Almost 50 years ago a crazy man went up into the tower with a crate full of firearms, and he began shooting at the people below, just as classes were getting out. Fourteen people were killed, 30-some wounded, and all the events of that day added another layer to the memory of the campus. The tower was open now for tours, and I was able to get over to the student union to sign up for one just as it was leaving.

When we came out on the observation deck, the people in our tour group—mostly nice white-haired ladies visiting from Dallas—all let out little gasps of pleasure, delight, surprise; I did, too. The west wind was blowing, and the city looked shiny and busy, a bit hazy with smog at the horizons.

I walked slowly around the deck. To the east were the red-tiled roofs of older university buildings, the flat industrial roofs of more recent structures, and beyond, the great hulk of the football stadium. The stadium was another link to the past: for years it had been known as Memorial Stadium, in memory of the WWI dead; in recent years the name had been hyphenated with that of a legendary former coach. A different memory performance. Further east, beyond the stadium, were the traditional African American neighborhoods, which were rapidly being gentrified; Anglofied; displaced.

To the north the city stretched endlessly, gray-roofed apartment buildings poking up above the trees forever and ever, on and on. Right below the tower to the west was the Undergraduate Library, and I again thought of Tom down in the basement. In the cellar: I had a brief Bachelardian flash, picturing Tom in the cellar of the university's house, and me—temporarily, at least—in the garret. What kind of dream would that make? How did that locate our lives? No idea. I looked farther to the west, across Guadalupe, and the neighborhood where students once lived in tumbledown old houses had in recent years been replaced by condos and luxury apartments. Beyond that, the heavy trees of Tarrytown; and beyond that, across the river and out of sight, my home.

"Isn't this just wonderful?" An old lady was standing next to me. The breeze pulled at her stiff white hair and her sunglasses glinted the sun at me. "I haven't been up here in so long!"

"It was closed for a long time," I said.

The lady laughed. "Oh, I was here a long, long time ago—before you were born. I graduated in nineteen-sixty-three."

"It must've been a different city then," I said.

"I used to live down there somewhere." She pointed down at West Campus and laughed again. Cheerful. "We drove around yesterday looking for where I lived, and I don't think the street is even there anymore."

"Everything changes here," I said. Then I thought: Well, things change everywhere—things in Austin just change faster. Then I wondered if that was true. Maybe it was, and maybe it wasn't. The changes that occurred were sort of layered, so that the past was always there, if you could dig it up...or maybe more like a palimpsest, something you could read if you looked at it correctly....

"Such a view," the lady said.

But maybe if the city was always changing—if change was the normal state—then it never really changed at all.

It was a place always in a constant process of becoming.

The lady said, "Beautiful...."

Just below me to the south were the Confederate statues and the South Mall. I thought of the people the sniper shot, death from above. Wow. Behind me on the face of the clock tower there were gouges from the impact of bullets fired back at the sniper—and sniper died here, too, killed on this very deck. Another layer of death and memory. Beyond the mall the art museum loomed up, a handsome building. Across MLK Blvd, the State Museum of Texas, various state office buildings and the capitol, shining in the afternoon sun. Further, the towers of downtown, Clayton's office down there. He had quite a view, too.

I hit a phone button and called Clayton. He answered on the second ring

26.

"Oh, so you're hanging up on me now?"

"I'm sorry," I said.

"Sure—"

"Hey, I'm on top of the Texas Tower," I said. "I can see all the way to your house!"

"What a good idea!" The old lady was standing next to me again. She pulled a silver flip phone from her purse and punched away at the keys, drifting away a little bit to give me—or herself—some privacy.

Clayton didn't say anything. Before the heart attack he might have flirted, a little. If I'd said I could see all the way to his house, he might have said that he was walking around naked. Could I see his pecker? But now there was silence.

"You've lived here forever, right?" I knew Clayton was from Houston, originally, had come to Austin for his undergraduate degree—in English—and had then gone on to the law school. Then to Cox O'Brien. "Have you ever been up here?"

"No," Clayton said. "You've done something I haven't done. Congratulations."

Grumpy.

"I didn't mean it like that! I was just thinking that you could—you should—come up here with me sometime. You could tell me what I'm looking at."

"Yeah, maybe."

The old lady said, "I can see all the way to Dallas!" Except she was looking toward San Antonio.

"What're you doing?" I asked Clayton.

"Sitting here with my dog, watching Dr. Phil on TV. They've got this woman they call the Bitch of the Year on. She treats everybody like shit."

"Ah." I thought of Clayton sitting there with Scumbo. Animals are usually good for cheering people up, but Clayton sounded depressed. "Listen," I said. "I've got to go. See you tonight?"

"Yeah," Clayton said. "Whatever."

27.

I hit disconnect, then the key for my camera. I took two or three pictures of the South Mall and the city beyond. Then I walked around the observation deck taking shots from the east, the north, and the west. Then, as I looked out toward my home, I realized that I was at the center of the city. Not quite literally, as in the center of a perfect circle—vast, irregular neighborhoods stretched out to the northwest and southeast— but I was at the center of the city morally and psychically: I was at the center pivot of the city's dynamo, the source of everything good and bad, all the energy on display, all the money that flowed into the city, all the layers of memory. It wasn't the state government that was responsible for Austin, the city as it existed, it was the university. Everything I could see was created by the university—by the hundreds of thousands of active, energetic young people who had passed through it, by the hundreds of thousands who stayed in Austin, at least for a little while, building this intricate web of homes and businesses and schools and stores—of life— the web stretching out to the working class households of the north and east and south, an economic web that brought employment at second and third and fourth removes to thousands and thousands of people. The university, oligarchic and corporate, had brought all this into being, doing its best to if not transcend at least ignore the miserable treasonous foundation displayed on the South Mall. Morally, everything in Austin belonged to the university; everything in Austin belonged to knowledge.

The tour guides were ready to go back down again, and I followed them into the elevator. When the door closed, I turned and asked, "Is there a monument anywhere on campus to the people that got shot?

"At the Turtle Pond," a guide said. "Just north of the tower."

On the ground again, I went out through the north door, through a little courtyard, across a parking lot, and over to the Turtle Pond. Red-eared turtles basked on rocks under the bright sun. Students lounged around with books and laptops. A tiny brass plaque mentioned tragedy and sorrow but didn't bother to list the names of the dead. A grudging memory, it seemed. A miserable sad attempt at public forgetting. I took a few photos, then walked around the corner and stood looking up at the old Littlefield House, a giant, turreted old Victorian pile, the former home of Major Littlefield.

28.

Clayton was still sitting in his pajamas gazing at the television when I got to his house in the evening. Scumbo greeted me at the door, excited and happy, then hopped back up on Clayton's lap. I went over and kissed Clayton on the top of his head.

"C'mon," I said. "Help me go shopping."

I had volunteered to make dinner for Clayton and Andrea the next day or so, and I knew he didn't have anything in the house except for frozen pizzas and scotch.

"I'm watching SportsCenter," Clayton said.

There's no arguing with a depressed person; reason won't move them. You have to tell them what to do.

"SportsCenter will be on later," I said. "I need you to do this with me, now."

Clayton took his time dressing but eventually came slowly down the stairs looking presentable and followed me slowly out to my car. We drove past his local grocery store and got on the expressway, heading north.

"That's a perfectly good store back there," Clayton said.

"You need to get out and drive around."

"Well, shit. I'd rather stay at home and watch SportsCenter or some basketball."

"I really liked going up on the Tower today," I said. "I'd like you to go up there with me sometime."

"I might jump off."

I glanced at Clayton. He wasn't suicidal—was he?

"They have a big fence up there, so you can't get over the edge—so *people* can't get over the edge."

Clayton sat staring at the traffic straight ahead. "Yeah," he said, "well, a few months ago some teacher jumped off the back of the football stadium."

"I heard about that," I said. The unfortunate now-famous adjunct who was depressed about grading. "You don't have his reason to jump."

"When I was a student some kid jumped out an open window at the Architecture Building."

"That building was obviously poorly designed," I said. "You're not jumping anywhere."

Clayton sighed. "I have to go back to work next week."

I thought of his office on the 19th floor: he was used to dramatic views. Though perhaps not from the center; perhaps his view was lopsided, out of kilter. Or maybe mine was.

"That'll be fun," I said. "You get to get dressed and go back to work! Everybody's going to be so happy to see you."

"I suppose," Clayton said. Then he said, "I've got all this work to do, and I just don't want to do any of it."

I exited at Lamar Boulevard and began driving north. "Okay," I said, "You've lived here forever, right? So tell me what's different—tell me what wasn't here when you went to college."

"I don't know." Clayton sagged a little. "Everything—it's all different."

"Tell me," I said. "I want to know about Austin. I've lived

here almost six years and I don't know anything."

"Read a book," Clayton said.

"There's not much out there." Fictional treatments, Austin as setting, in Brammer's *The Gay Place*, or Hynes's *Kings of Infinite Space*, or *Next*, or White's *That Demon Life*, but I couldn't find a nonfiction book that narrated Austin, that explained what it was or what it meant. I was beginning to think that maybe I should write one.

We were coming up on a used bookstore.

"That used to be a nightclub," Clayton said.

"Good—that's what I want. Tell me more."

There was a closed building that used to be barbecue restaurant that used to be a seafood restaurant. A place where a bar burned down. Clayton could remember some things if he wanted to. A stoplight that used to be a four-way stop. A Mexican restaurant that used to be a Pizza Hut. We stopped at a red light.

"I went to a party back there once." Clayton pointed at an apartment complex back behind the Mexican restaurant. "There was a kid there, this Korean kid, he'd been adopted by a family from Muleshoe, of all places—he had the damndest accent you ever heard."

"Okay, good."

"He had a summer job as a bible salesman. No shit. Jazz fan, too—he told me all about Keith Jarrett."

"Yeah?" The light changed and I began driving north again.

"I don't know why I remember that kid."

"He was interesting," I said.

Clayton pointed across the street. "There used to be a house next to that restaurant where I bought pot once."

"Good!" I said. "This is what I want to know." The past gives depth to location, even if it's someone else's past. "What else?"

"Oh, shit, I don't know." Clayton was looking out the window and shaking his head. Sad. "Everything's different now. Everything's all about money. The whole city." He looked over at me. "What the fuck are you trying to do, Camille? Talking about all this shit is depressing. I just had a heart attack—I'm dying."

I reached over and patted him on the knee. "You just need to think in terms of memory," I said.

"Memory?" Clayton asked. "Please. You're an English professor, not a historian."

29.

In class we were looking at paintings by George Catlin, portraits of tribes of the northern plains, and reading James Welch's *Fools Crow*, a novel set among the Blackfeet in the mid-19th century. Discussion had been a little sluggish in recent classes, so I forced the students to speak, going around the seminar table counterclockwise, each student obligated to speak for 90 seconds, minimum.

Most began, "Well, I liked..." and then would ramble on for a bit. They liked different things: some of them liked the Catlin painting where the women are crossing the frozen Missouri River to gather firewood, and some of them liked the action scenes in *Fools Crow,* and so forth. It was an undergraduate class, and most students found it difficult to get past the autobiographical "I liked" or "I didn't like" to examine what it was about the work they liked, or didn't. That was always a problem. But they all said something. Even Travis Sherwood, who always came to class late and half-hungover, looked up from his notebook to say that he liked the part in *Fools Crow* where the Blackfeet encounter a domestic housecat for the first time.

"That's a nice detail," I said. I try to be encouraging. "So, what does that say about cultural perspectives, if anything?"

"Uh, that they're different?" Travis looked perplexed, and tired. "I don't know—that cats aren't native to North America?"

Close enough. Travis sat at the far right end of the table. Across from him, at the far left corner of the table, sat Nelda Krueger. Nelda was looking down at her phone.

"Nelda," I said. "Your turn. Ninety seconds."

Nelda blushed. "Uh, I guess I'm just wondering why everybody makes such a big deal about Indians."

I looked at her. I thought, Oh, no. But I said, "Okay. Keep going...."

Nelda shrugged. "All you ever do is see them whining on TV. I mean, they've got casinos, right?"

A couple of students laughed. I just stared at her.

"They're *poor*," Travis said.

"True," I said. "You have to remember that reservations are some of the poorest places in the country."

"So?" Nelda asked. "They just need to go out and get jobs. Like anyone else on welfare."

"They *can't* get jobs," Travis said. "There aren't any jobs on reservations."

"So?" Nelda asked. "Then they need to go to where there *are* jobs. Just like anyone else on welfare!"

"But—" Travis was starting to get worked up. "But— they've all been genocided and had their land stolen—"

"That was a long time ago. I think they need to stop whining about that. I didn't take their land." Nelda was starting to get worked up, too. She'd been almost silent all semester; until now. "And what about those casinos? *I'd* like to have a casino!"

I said, "About the book...."

"Oh—I haven't finished it yet. But—I liked the cat thing, too." Nelda nodded at Travis.

"The paintings?" I asked.

"They're okay." Nelda looked up at the screen. A painting showing a buffalo hunt was up on the screen, buffalo stampeding off to the right, an Indian on horseback in pursuit. "They're okay. I like them."

"Excellent," I said. At some point in teaching, with some students, you have to give up on the idea that they'll achieve any sort of ability to think critically, that they will be able to transcend the prejudices they've grown up with. Teacher can't compete with mom and dad and preacher, with television;

with the culture. Sometimes, with some students, yes; with other students, no. With Nelda, I suspected, no. There's no use fighting a lost cause.

I looked at the next student. "So, Jason? What are you thinking?"

Jason said something about liking something. I wasn't paying attention. I did see Nelda smile at Travis. What was that about? A little romance? Unlikely. Travis was a mess. Then the bell rang and class ended. I called Nelda over.

"Am I in trouble?" she asked. She sat down at the corner of the table, at my left.

"What?"

"About what I said? About the Indians?"

"Oh—no." I try not to take seriously the seriously the opinions of 18 year-olds about anything social or political. I listen to what they say, but I don't take them seriously. "I was just worried about this." I pushed the essay proposal across the table to her.

"Oh," Nelda said. "What's wrong with it?"

"Well," I said, "you could be—should be—a little more detailed. Well, a lot more detailed."

"I'm writing my paper about what we talk about in class—people moving west."

"That's very broad. Also there were already people living in the west."

"Oh," Nelda said. "So it *is* about the Indians, huh?"

I said, "You need to be more specific in your proposal."

"Oh." Nelda glanced at the proposal and then looked up at me. "Cowboys?"

"Try focusing on one of the artists we're been talking about, or one of the authors," I said. "If you're interested in Native Americans, maybe you could write your paper on Welch or Alexie or Silko."

"I'm not really interested in Indians," Nelda said. "I just think they need to get jobs and stop whining."

I looked at her. I just felt really sad.

"I guess I'm pretty conservative, huh?" Nelda flashed her

wet white smile at me.

Yes, I thought. That—or racist. But.

"I just—I just think you need to be more specific on your paper," I said. "You need to be more specific on your topic, and you kind of need to tell me what your argument's going to be. You need to tell me what it all means, right?"

I was afraid she was going to tell me that it meant "they" needed to get jobs or something. To stop whining. But she just took her stupid proposal and stuck it in her notebook.

"Okay," Nelda said. "I'll come up with something."

Another inward sigh for me. Okay, she said. You tell some kids what to do, how to improve their writing, and they say Okay, and nod, and their eyes are dead or scared or resentful and they can't wait to get away, even though you're trying to help them. Okay? Okay. Okay! Her loss.

"Your paper counts for 50% of your grade," I said. "I want you to succeed in this class. Okay?"

Nelda said, "Okay."

30.

On the way back to my office I ducked into the mailroom to see if any more useless memos had come through. I found Wytowski in there with a pair of undergraduate girls tacking up big sheets of paper to the wall.

"What's all this?" I asked. "Your art project?"

"It's going to be nice," Wytowski said.

I kind of doubted it. The stained walls of the room still had those pale rectangles where the Dead Professors had been hanging for so many years. The pale rectangles peeked out from under the white sheets of paper and reinforced the shabbiness of the room.

"This one's so cute!" One of the undergrad girls held up a crayon drawing of a blue house, a yellow, ray-emitting sun, and a pair of happy stick-figure people standing outside the house. Also a four-legged stick-figure; a dog, maybe, or a cat.

"I'm sure it will cheer everyone up," I said. Wytowski frowned; no doubt he detected a trace of sarcasm. I didn't care. I didn't care for the artwork of kids, either; or for kids, period. One thing I have never, ever, regretted is my lack of children; dogs, yes; cats, yes, of course. But no kids. They're noisy, dirty, distracting, expensive, time-consuming—and bad artists, too. I asked Wytowski, "But aren't you worried about privileging parents over non-parents?"

"So far, no one's complained," Wytowski said.

The girl tacked the drawing up. Wytowski held up another: a finger painting of blue and purple blobs.

"Charming," I said.

Wytowski faced the wall and stuck a push-pin in the corner of the painting. He asked, "Have you read the EDSAP report yet?"

"I've looked through it," I said.

"What we're trying to do, you know, is to increase the overall accessibility of the English Department," Wytowski said. "Right, Carolyn?"

He touched the girl on the shoulder.

"Right!" Carolyn said.

"Accessibility's fine," I said. I sat my books down and leafed through the paintings and drawings: houses, people, dogs, cats, cars; blobs. Privileging kids over adults. I said, "We have to look to the future, right?"

31.

I was standing in Clayton's kitchen that evening, alone, surrounded by various bubbling and steaming pots, when I heard the front door open. Clayton was in the front room, watching television with Scumbo, and the little dog began barking happily. I heard voices and walked around the corner to find Andrea standing in the entryway with another woman.

"Hi," I said.

Clayton hobbled in from the front room. "Oh," he said. He looked at me—frowned at me. "This is Sallie."

Sallie, Clayton's first wife.

"Well, you're up and about!" Sallie said to Clayton.

"Sort of," Clayton said. He turned and wobbled back to

the TV. Andrea slunk along after him.

"Well," Sallie said. She beamed at me with sort of the sad gray coffee-stained teeth so common to academics. "You must be Camille."

"Yep," I said. "You want a drink? A glass of wine?" It's been my experience that potentially uncomfortable situations are helped by alcohol—any sort of alcohol—and so I opened another bottle of Chilean cabernet and poured Sallie a big glass. Drinking would give her something to do while I finished dinner: grilled salmon marinated in rum, brown rice, butternut squash puree, and big wads of broccoli.

"I've heard so much about you," Sallie said.

"Really?" I asked. Clayton had never talked much about his exes, except to mention their existence: Sallie, mother of Andrea, who taught composition at ACC, and Laura, an associate professor at UT-San Antonio who specialized in children's lit. I didn't really know anything about Sallie, and had never been curious enough to ask about her.

"Andrea's been telling me how you're been taking care of Clayton," Sallie said. "It's good somebody is—he's never been able to take care of himself."

I didn't say anything. Was I taking care of Clayton?

"He's always been halfway helpless—more than halfway. I still don't think he knows how to do his own laundry."

"That's why there's cleaners," I said.

"We couldn't afford cleaners back when we were first married." Sallie leaned back against the kitchen counter and sipped at her wine. "I don't know how many tons of dirty laundry I lugged down to the Kwik-Wash when we were in grad school."

I didn't say anything. I wasn't going to be disloyal. I didn't know who this woman was, really; and I had no reason to trust her. The grill was hot and I took the salmon fillets and tonged them on, droplets of marinade sizzling and smoke rising to the fan.

I said, "Clayton's done pretty well, I think."

"Oh, he's just a big baby," Sallie said.

32.

Clayton came in unwillingly from the front room and sat at the head of the table, with Andrea on his right, and Sallie on his left. I brought in plates, two at a time, and then bottles of wine. I sat at the end of the table, facing Clayton.

"Everything looks so good!" Sallie said to me.

I shrugged. Now that I was finished, I found that I didn't really care. I sat and watched them talk to each other, realizing the basic futility of families. They didn't really do anything for anyone. In the end I guess that is why I was—and am—such a poor writer of creative non-fiction: most memoirs are about families, and I had nothing to say about families except to express annoyance at their dullnesses. I didn't have anything against my parents, or against the family I married into; they were all nice-enough people, and I wished them all well. I was 24 years-old in graduate school when I was trying to write a memoir, and I didn't have a daddy who'd abused me, or a mommy who was domineering; no alcoholism, no craziness, no color. I tried to write a memoir, but it didn't work. It could be, too, that I just didn't know how to write about life. This is all I knew about me: that I grew up wanting to read books and look at pictures and avoid people—my parents, my husband, my classmates. I didn't want to hang out with anyone. That never changed. Right now, especially, I didn't want to hang around with Clayton and his boring family. Or even with Clayton by himself, really; not anymore.

"This is better than hospital food," Clayton said.

"Well, that's high praise," I said. Sallie laughed.

"It's good," Clayton said. He looked at Sallie. "You didn't even come to see me in the hospital."

"I didn't even know you were in the hospital until you were almost out!" Sallie said. She pointed at Andrea. "This one didn't tell me."

Andrea shrugged; pouty. I don't think she liked being around her parents any more than I did.

I remembered a trip Clayton and I took in the fall, to Tacoma for a meeting of the Western Literature Association.

I sat in the window seat on the flight, Clayton in the middle, and on the aisle was a young man, an attorney who was heading to Seattle for a job interview. I fell asleep while Clayton and the lawyer talked about law and job interviews and people they sort of knew in common. I slept until the approach to Seattle when the jet hit some turbulence and I jolted awake to hear the young man screaming, "Jesus-God-we're-going-down!" Clayton looked at me, surprised, and I looked past him at the lawyer, who was all panicked and red in the face. The plane jolted again and he screamed again, screaming "We're going DOWN!" so loud that some GIs, members of the Alaska National Guard on their way home from Afghanistan, woke up from their exhausted sleep and stared at him in wonder. At the hotel in Tacoma, we'd been promised a room with a view of Mt. Rainier, but all we could see were the low, depressing, stratus clouds that hung over the city, the gloomy city and the gloomy forests of the northwest. Each morning I would look out the window, only to be disappointed at the clouds and the gloom. Where was the mountain? It was a cruel hoax. Clayton would laugh and grab me around the waist, drag me back to bed. "We're going down!" he'd yell. "We're going doooooooooooown!" We stayed in that room the whole time, leaving only so that I could present my paper on drought narrative, and, then, on the last evening, we got dressed and went up to the hotel's top-floor bar. A group of GI medics from Ft. Lewis were in the banquet room, celebrating their safe return from the war: hard, tired-looking young men in dress uniforms with their dates in formal dresses. One soldier was with a tall woman with flowing black hair who wore a lovely warm red gown cut low on her back, exposing a near-life-size tattoo of a mermaid. The soldier grasped her hand tight and pulled her close, even though she moved away a little, just a little, and he reached out to touch the mermaid, and she flinched. I sat there solemnly watching them, knowing that they would not be long together. Clayton looked at them, too, smiling, and he said, "Aw, they're just like us."

33.

Clayton ate with some appetite, but he didn't touch his broccoli.

"Here I thought you were the king of broccoli," I said.

He shrugged. "I can't eat it."

"You never liked broccoli," Sallie said.

"Broccoli interferes with that warfarin I'm taking—with my blood thinners," Clayton said. He pushed the plate away. "I thought everybody knew that."

"Clayton's never been much for vegetables," Sallie said to me, a loud whisper.

"Some people change," Clayton said.

"Most people don't." Sallie dropped her last bite of salmon to Scumbo.

Silence. I filled my wineglass.

"So, Dad," Andrea said. "What was it like? When you died? Did you see the white light?"

"He didn't die," I said.

"My heart stopped for ten minutes," Clayton said. "I guess that's dead."

I didn't say anything; I sat and remembered. He'd collapsed just as I entered the examining room, and I remembered how they stretched him out on the gurney with his big white belly sticking up and all the doctors and nurses and techs scrambling around, and I remember how they pushed me out of the room while they readied the paddles, and I remember how guilty I'd felt, like it was my fault for being disloyal, for wanting to be alone.

"And did you see the white light?"

"No," Clayton said. "There's nothing over there. Nothing. It's just black."

Sallie filled her glass again. "You're so cheerful."

"She asked me a question. I told her the truth."

"Maybe you weren't dead long enough," Andrea said. "Maybe you were in the dark before the light."

"You're thinking in clichés," Clayton said. "I've warned you about that. You need to think for yourself." He looked at

Sallie. "What're you teaching these kids?"

"Me?" Sallie laughed.

"These kids today don't read books," Clayton said. "What're you doing to get them to like literature?"

"Some people are visual," Andrea said. "Some people don't like literature."

"Some people don't try."

"Wait—are you talking about me?" Andrea asked. "I read books!"

"Vampire books don't count."

"I don't know," I said. Really, I don't know why I was trying to keep the peace. "Some of those vampire books can be interesting, at least from a cultural point of view."

"You're looking at it like an English professor."

"I am—"

"Not a *reader*," Clayton said. "Not an adult reader. Those are books for little kids."

"I'm happy when my students read anything," Sallie said.

"And you're not even an English teacher," Clayton said to her. "You're a composition teacher." He sat silent a long time, pushing around the broccoli on his plate, and then he said, "And I was too dead."

34.

I got an email from Ralph asking me to stop by his office, and when I got there I found him sitting with Ken Wytowski.

"Have you finished EDSAP yet?" Wytowski asked, even before I sat down.

"No—I'm still working on it," I said. I sounded like a student. How annoying. His bugging me about EDSAP was getting annoying, too.

"Have you read my special section on computer-enhanced education and distance learning?"

"—No, not really."

"Well," Ralph said. "Well, I wanted to ask you something." I saw that he had my syllabus on his desk, the syllabus for the western narratives class. He held it up. "You're teaching this again next spring, correct?"

"Something like it," I said. "I might play with the reading list a little."

Wytowski asked, "And you're aware of the emphasis ED-SAP puts on interactive, customer-based education?"

"Yeah...." I was waiting for something; something bad.

"So," Ralph said, "we're wondering if you would volunteer to teach this class as an online class."

An online class. Fuck no, I thought. I asked, "Why?"

"Two reasons," Ralph said. He leaned back in his chair and pointed his beard at me. "One, you're highly respected in this department, and your participation in the implementation of the EDSAP pilot would set a great example for everyone."

"A great example," Wytowski echoed.

"Second," Ralph said, "your class has a very impressive visual component that could be transported and shared quite easily in an online environment."

"All those paintings," Wytowski said. "Wouldn't they be great to look at online?"

"They're already on my website," I said.

"See? You're halfway there already!"

I thought of my students: odd and strange and distant and mysterious, like all people. But sometimes you could see them make a connection; see them get what you were teaching. Sitting in a dim room and talking about books was the best thing there ever was. How could you do that on a computer?

I said, "Online...."

"That's the goal," Wytowski said. "I'm predicting that we can move maybe three-quarters of our classes online, and then we can increase enrollment without increasing the size of the physical plant."

I'd read enough of the report to know that was only part of it: they were also planning on letting the numbers of tenured faculty dwindle through attrition, until all that was left of the department was a few well-paid administrators and handful of ancient doddering silverback professors and a mob of sickly adjunct serfs. My problem was that I wasn't tenured—yet. They could dwindle me any time they wanted. Once I got inside, I'd be fairly safe; perhaps.

"We think distance instruction is going to be especially effective in text-intensive classes," Ralph said. "And visual-intensive classes, too."

What the fuck. Text-intensive and visual-intensive: what other kinds of classes were there?

35.

At home I sat in my office and looked at the walls. For the book I'd just finished, the one on the literature of drought and memory in the Southwest, I had decorated the walls with dozens of photographs: dust storms approaching, dead cattle, dried lakes and playas, wilted lawns. They gave me something to think about while I wrote. But now that book was off at OU Press, and it was time to start on something new. I got up and began tearing down the drought pictures: tearing down, it didn't matter if they ripped, they were just things I had printed off my computer, all the raging deadly dust clouds and creekbeds baking under the sun. I took them down. The cats sat in the doorway, watching me. I filled a trash bag with wadded-up paper.

Then I started printing out the photos I'd taken of the South Mall: Robert E. Lee, Albert Sidney Johnston, the others. The Confederates. The Traitors. Then my pictures from the top of the tower: the city stretching off and off into the smoggy distance, all that space and place, those busy people, everything and everyone caught in a moment of transition, all in the process of becoming something else, something new. I printed off some old photographs of Austin I'd found on the internet: parades, policemen, political rallies; tornados and floods. I printed them all off and stuck them to my office walls. Then I turned to the kitties.

"This is where we live," I said. They just looked at me. How nice. There's nothing wrong about living alone with a houseful of books and a few interesting cats.

I sat back down at my computer and wrote a sentence.

To experience place is to participate in *memory*.

Well. I wasn't really sure if that was true or not, or even half-true, but it was enough writing for one day. I had a few years of reading to do.

36.

Dr. Lonnie Sezler was famous: he had been interviewed by Oprah. Charlie Rose, too, and he'd been on C-SPAN a couple of times, but Oprah was what everyone in the Department was talking about: an academic who'd been on Oprah! An academic who was almost famous—the inventor of the Pastoral University!

I wasn't impressed when I first saw him: a slender man in an expensive, shiny, olive-colored suit, his thick wavy hair swept back across the top of his head; standing at the front of the room, talking to Ralph and Wytowski and the Department Chair, he looked slick and unreliable. There were other big shots up there with him, too: the chancellor, and the chair of the board of regents, and several other white men in suits. The Dr. Lonnie lecture was a special event, so it was being held in the art museum, on the second floor, in a vast, high-ceilinged room filled with contemporary art installations and glass sculptures. Tiny folding chairs had been set up in a semicircle facing the podium, with a couple of rows of benches behind the chairs, and a few sofas behind the benches. I took a seat on one of the uncomfortable benches toward the rear of the room, and a little off to the side; as far away from the action as I could get and still be present. Really, I had better things to do than to be introduced to the Pastoral University.

Dru Hastings came in and plopped down next to me; heaving. She peered into her massive briefcase and said, "Are we happy to be here?"

I wasn't sure if she was talking to me or to her notebooks, but I said, "I've heard he's been on Oprah!"

Dru looked over to me and smiled. "I've heard that, too—I've heard he's very inspirational! I've heard that the Pastoral University will save us all."

I doubted that. I'd read Dr. Lonnie's book, *The Coming Pastoral University*, read it carefully, and I knew that the pastoral university was nothing but a big lie. It engendered visions of kindly shepherds reciting poetry to gentle flocks of sheep grazing amid the rolling green hills of Arcadian Academia. But a more close reading showed that the green rolling hills were not a commons but a property, and the shepherds poorly paid employees in constant danger of being supplanted by even more poorly-paid adjunct shepherds, and the sheep were not just sheared, but sheared and then sent to a slaughterhouse, and then devoured, and the owners of the property—owners of the shepherds, owners of the sheep— were not people but wolves. It was all a big lie.

My phone vibrated and I looked at it. Clayton.

r we on fr tomrrw?

Before his heart attack, we'd sort of made plans to go for a drive in the Hill Country over the weekend, to look at bluebonnets, to stay at a nice bed and breakfast in Kerrville. Now, for some reason, he said he still wanted to go, and I was trying to put him off. I was running out of patience with Clayton. I punched some buttons, texted him back.

I'm in a meeting right now.

Then a vibration; an answer.

If ur in a mting y r u txtng me

Oh, Clayton. Speak English. I put the phone down. Dru was watching me.

"You're getting to be like a student, huh?" Dru had a tight little black Moleskine notebook perched open on her big thigh; apparently she was a traditionalist.

Around us the room was filling, and the chairs and benches were quickly taken, and people began sitting on the floor. Our department was a large one, and even after almost six years there were many people I didn't know well; or at all. Older professors, younger grad students, men, women: Dr. Lonnie was getting a big turnout.

The Chair and Wytowski took seats in the front room and Ralph stepped up to the microphone and tapped on it two or three times. "Can you hear me?" he asked. People ignored him. "Is this working?"

"Poor Ralph," Dru said.

Ralph said something else, but one of the art installations began making noise: just behind the podium was a giant wall of video screens, dozens of them, showing, at first, blue skies. Then a bird would appear in one of the screens—a great-tailed grackle, I could always identify a grackle, they were the most common bird in Austin, a big bird, dinosaur-like, iridescent black with shiny yellow eyes and jutting fan-shaped tails— and then another grackle, and another, until all the screens were filled with black birds. Then they began making noise— croaking, hissing, chirping—louder and louder, until they finally took off flying in a sonic blast of ruffling feathers and flapping wings. Either someone forgot to turn off the installation, or they were unable to turn it off. When the birds were making noise, no one could hear anything.

"Thank you," Ralph said when the birds flew away. Everyone laughed. But I'd been to the museum just a few weeks ago, and I knew the birds would be back: the installation cycled through at random times every few minutes. Ralph said, "Okay, I'd like to welcome you all to our inaugural EDSAP Lecture—"

"Inaugural," Dru said to me. "There's going to be more of these things?"

Ralph said a few more words about EDSAP. I played with my phone. My Facebook profile said I had 293 friends; that sounded about right. Most of them I had never met face-to-face, of course; and I liked that. I liked the idea of Facebook friends: people you didn't have to hang around with.

Clayton texted again.

You still havent tld me if were on fr wknd

We weren't on for anything. People were applauding: I looked up, and Dr. Lonnie was stepping to the podium. He was smiling a dazzling bright electric bleached white smile.

"I'm so glad," he said. "So very glad to be here."

Dru scribbled something in her notebook, and tilted it to show me.

He ought to be glad—we're paying him $14k!

Up front, Dr. Lonnie was leaning over the podium; it looked like he was making eye contact with the important people in the front row. Behind him the screens were quickly filling with grackles.

"What we're going to concentrate on today," Dr. Lonnie said, "is the future—"

The grackles started making noise. Dr. Lonnie kept talking, smiling out at everyone, never acknowledging the grackles.

Dru showed me her notebook.

The future is for the birds!

Then the birds all flew away—

"...and, as we gaze into the interminable, infinite, multi-discursive future, what do we see? Huh? Whom do we encounter?" Dr. Lonnie paused; excited, grinning. "Ourselves! Right? We'll be looking back, trying to understand the mess our past *selves* have made, trying to understand the situation we've gotten our*selves* of the future into!" The birds were cycling fast this time: grackles were popping up on screen after screen. "No matter what we do today, no matter what we do now, it'll be a future mystery for our future *selves* to solve and understand!"

Dru wrote:

Huh?

I took the notebook from her and wrote.

the past is unwritten

Dru wrote:

It's another country

I wrote:

what is the future?

Dru wrote:

Not ours!

Clayton texted:

Im reading that mcmurtry book u gave me, he had a bad heart too!

Dr. Lonnie said, "...by clinging to a text-based worldview, we have, of course, anchored ourselves to a dying culture...."

The birds started making noise again. Down front, the Chair leaned over to Ralph and said something. Ralph got up and walked around the side of the room and headed for the back; he passed right by Dru and myself, but didn't say anything. I turned and watched him go out the door.

Dru wrote:

I thought he was going to bust us!

I wrote:

what's he going to do—make us clean chalkboards?

Actually, only the older buildings had chalkboards anymore. But whatever.

At the podium, Dr. Lonnie kept on talking, despite the grackles. He spread his arms and tilted his head to the side: a martyr, a Christ. The birds flew away with a roar. Dr. Lonnie said, "We must refuse this outcome!"

Dru didn't write anything. She just looked over at me, astonished.

The light in the room dimmed, and two large projection screens slowly descended from the ceiling behind Dr. Lonnie, covering the grackle installation.

"The fuck," I said. "PowerPoint?"

A pair of grad students in front of me turned around and grinned. I looked at my phone: no emails.

"Everybody hates literature," Dr. Lonnie said. "And, if we're honest, we'll admit that we hate literature, too."

Dru just stared at him. I just stared at him.

"All you rhetoric people, all you creative writing people, you literature people, all you engineers and biologists, and physicists and historians and philosophers—you all hate literature. Everybody—everybody in this room!—wishes that literature would go away." Dr. Lonnie smiled at us with his glittering toothy smile. "And it *is* going to go away. And we're going to go away with it!"

Ralph came back around the room and sat again at the front. He whispered something to the chair and shrugged his shoulders. Just then the birds started up again—hissing, croaking. A pair of old professors, old white men with big saggy bellies sitting up front in the row behind the Chair, got up and left.

Dru wrote:

They're taking literature with them!

The birds flew away, fluttery feathery sounds; then silence. Dr. Lonnie looked out at us—made eye contact with me, it seemed like. He said, "This is a *good* thing—"

On the screen behind Dr. Lonnie to stage left a simple white tombstone appeared, a white tombstone on a green field. On the stage right screen, white words on black: "Death of Text." Then there were two white tombstones on the left screen, then more. One the right, more words:"Death of Author." "Death of Teacher." "Death of Student." "Death of University." "Death of Knowledge." And more tombstones; more, until the left screen looked like one of the old military cemeteries in France, with the dead men planted row on row in identical graves. Then the screens faded to black.

Then a painting came up: Thomas Cole's "The Course of Empire, The Savage State." Cole was a painter I often used in my classes; I loved his wonderful dreamy Romantic landscapes, the beauty of an Edenic world too often falling under the axes of progress.

I took Dru's notebook and wrote:

this is perverse!!!!!!!!!!

Dru wrote:

well, Sezler DOES look like a child molester!

"Sezler the Molester," I said aloud.

Behind the screens, grackles started hissing. Dr. Lonnie kept talking. I was glad I couldn't hear him. Sezler the fucking molester. The whole painting series came up on his screen: "The Pastoral or Arcadian State," "The Consummation of Empire," "Destruction," and "Desolation." The bad thing— the worst bad thing, among many, many, many bad things— was that the allegory sort of made sense, if you could see the university as an empire, could imagine its development, its destruction. I wished I'd thought of it first; though I wasn't sure what conclusion Dr. Lonnie was drawing from the paintings. Wytowski and Ralph looked entranced, so it was probably a load of shit.

My phone vibrated. Clayton.

r u still mtng?

I answered.

It's a lecture, not a meeting. I hate it!!!!

Clayton texted:

then leave

Other professors were leaving; old ones, for the most part. The audience left behind was now mostly younger professors and grad students; that is, people without power, people who were too afraid to leave. I don't know. I suppose I could have gotten up and walked away, and maybe I should have, but I would have had to step around or over Dru, and she seemed content to sit there, massive and wide, looking puzzled—or amused—blocking me. It was easier, really, to do nothing; to just sit there. I texted Clayton:

I'm trapped

The Incomplete

> What does education do? It makes a straight-
> cut ditch out of a free, meandering brook.
> —Henry David Thoreau

So there we were in jail, Barnes and myself, stuck in the same cell, on a charge of public intoxication, because of my genius, my brilliance: I watch a lot of TV, and I learn things, and I used that knowledge to talk Barnes out of a Driving While Intoxicated, and so—there we were, in jail, in a cell.

"The thing is." Barnes stopped. "The thing is, I hate the fucking cops."

"Of course!" Me. "They exist—they exist only to persecute the persecutable."

Barnes I knew had five or six DWIs already, most back in the old days, the seventies, back when he was my age and nobody gave a shit about drunk driving. Nowadays, in this prosecution-mad, vile age, he'd be in prison, and his hounds would be without anyone to feed them, and I'd be without a roommate.

"Punish the powerless!" Me.

"Fuck the cops." Barnes.

Up and down the hall—the cellblock, if that's what it was called, I didn't know the exact term, maybe cellblock was a prison term, and we were only in jail—up and down whatever it was, people were yelling: it was sort of like TV, sort of like the jail scenes in Tom Wolfe's *A Man in Full*, but not quite: it was a Monday night—Tuesday morning, now—and there weren't that many people locked up, surprisingly few, really, and we were in the cell, wearing our orange jail pajamas, listening to isolated yells from people up and down the tier, or whatever it was called. Across the hall or whatever was a black man in a cell—a pimp, Barnes said—who kept banging on his door and yelling, "Monique! Monique! You out there?" as if she could hear him all the way to wherever they were keeping the women prisoners. "Monique! Monique!"

"That was really smart, though." Barnes. "What you did with the cops."

Barnes and I had been playing pool and being cool until the bar closed and we decided to swing by Waitress Stacy's to see if she had any weed—all Barnes had was some crank back at the house—and we were headed to Stacy's and Barnes wasn't paying attention and ran a four-way stop, and there was a cop on the other side of the intersection. "Pull over!" I said. "Just pull over!" There was a plumbing supply shop on the other side of the street, on the corner, and Barnes pulled into the parking lot—he shut up and did what I told him to do, a miracle. "Let's just get out of the car," I said. "I saw this on TV—they won't know who's driving, they won't arrest both of us." It was something I'd seen on a cop show: a hood ended up outwitting a rookie cop and getting away without a DWI. And though my plan kept Barnes from getting a DWI— from probably going to prison, given his stupid record from back in ancient days—they did end up arresting both of us, for Public Intoxication. But since neither of us were holding anything, it was no big deal.

"Well, I'm really smart." Me. "You know? All that TV I watch, those books I read, music—"

"Fuck you." Barnes. "We're just lucky that cop tonight was as stupid as the one on TV."

"Ha!"

I stared at the ceiling above my bunk: nothing profound

with the graffiti, just some scrawls that I couldn't make out scratched into the paint, and what looked like a huge dangly cock. So this was jail: an experience I always needed to have, I thought, something I needed to see: though actually it was turning out to be kind of boring.

"Aren't we supposed to have a riot?" Me. "Aren't we supposed to fight the other prisoners or the guards? Aren't we supposed to shank a snitch? Aren't we supposed to get raped? Aren't we supposed to express our fucking dissatisfaction with this place? I mean—man, what the fuck?"

"I'm too old for more craziness." Barnes. He swung out of his bunk and dropped his pants and sat on the toilet. I rolled away and faced the wall, to give him some privacy— also, there were some jail experiences I didn't need to have.

"Actually, we do pretty well." Barnes. Grunting. "Tonight with the cops, and then at the murder."

Whoa: the murder! The sudden murder we'd witnessed five months earlier, a stabbing, we never talked about it. I don't think we were scared of it, all traumatized and disturbed: the wallowing in blood and gore, wearing bloody clothes all night to go talk to the fucking cops in the morning. Barnes just said he'd never talk about that night, and I just sort of followed his lead.

"We actually handled ourselves pretty well that night." Barnes sighed and flushed the toilet. "You'd think the cops would cut us some slack after we helped 'em out."

"We fingered the evil-doer." Me.

"Fucking cops."

: : : : :

Barnes got out of jail about two hours before I did, even though he got fined twice as much as I did and ordered to attend some sort of group counseling meeting—something to do with his history of alcohol-related offenses. The judge was a tired-faced sandy-haired woman who looked at him for a long time and finally said, "Mr. Barnes, you're obviously an alcoholic—you're just being ridiculous," and I know Barnes was thinking something like, "Yeah, and you're a stupid, menopausal bitch." But he didn't say anything, he kept his mouth shut for once, and the judge fussed at him and fined him and turned him loose, and then she fussed at me, and called me ridiculous, too, and she fined me and sent me back upstairs for two more boring hours. The jail was quiet in the morning, and cool, with only a few distant metallic bangings. I yelled, "Screws! Fucking screws!" But no jailers came to mess with me or beat me up, and I slept for a while until a turnkey actually did come and take me out of the cell and downstairs and let me get dressed in my clothes and gave me back my money and my cell phone, and dumped me out on the street in front of the jail in the bright spring sunshine. I sat on the curb to put on my shoes, blinking in the bright morning, and Barnes drove up in his car. I got in the car: there was a warm unopened 40-ounce bottle of malt liquor rolling around on the floor. I thought about opening it, but even though I was thirsty, I didn't.

"I can't believe they didn't tow the car." Barnes. He looked all frizzled gray and frazzled sitting there behind the wheel, smoking a cigarette. Tough, though, too, he looked: tough and tired.

"If they searched it, would they find anything?"

"Who knows." Barnes pulled out into traffic and crossed the river and went south, then off under some shady trees to an old slipshod bungalow on an old street where the other bungalows had mostly all been torn down and replaced with mansions and palaces. Barnes lived in the shabbiest house on the street—the only shabby house left on the street, really— and had lived there for almost 30 years, through all the changes and destruction that had happened in Austin.

When we got out of the car we could hear the hounds howling inside: the Barnes Hounds, Baby-Killer and Luddie, a pair of big long tawny dogs, some weird cross of German shepherd and basset and coonhound and who knew what else—loud crazy dogs. Barnes opened the front door—he never locked it—and the hounds bounded out and greeted Barnes grinning and dancing, then they took off racing around the balding splotchy yard, stopping to piss and shit, then racing back up—happy, happy, to see us.

"Aw, Baby-Killer!" Barnes, the hounds jumping at him. "Luddie, you missed me?"

I went in through the front room—the main room, where Barnes kept his old-fashioned stereo and his thousands of vinyl albums—back through the middle room, where Barnes slept with BK and Luddite, and back to my bedroom. Through a door, which I kept shut, to keep the hounds from eating my stuff, though I didn't have much. I kept it simple: bed, desk, computer, rack to hang my clothes on when I felt like hanging them, two or three big plastic tubs to keep clothes and miscellaneous junk safe. Miscellaneous junk: my assets. At the bottom of a big green tub, under my socks, was a little plastic pouch of methamphetamine, crank, and I found that and laid out a fat little line and sucked it up my nose with the red plastic husk of an old ink pen. Crank::::::::::::and the fine bitter taste washed down the back of my throat::::::::::::::::oh oh oh oh yes—

Outside Barnes sat on the porch watching the hounds nose around the yard. He looked at them happily, with love, flicking cigarette ashes into the dry gray grass.

"Look at those babies." Barnes. "They're beautiful."

"You're off today, right?" Me.

"Thank god for days off." Barnes was manager of low-rent a pawnshop, and spent six days a week arguing with people about the value of their miserable possessions.

"I've got to go to class." Me.

"Like that?"

I looked down, at my clothes, at my Me: I was all dirty and I probably smelled like jail.

"I'll take a shower."

"Jesus, kid—get some sleep, take a day off."

The bathroom floor next to the toilet was all rotted away from years of Barnes missing the bowl, but the tub and shower worked::::::::::::::::::::::and I stood under the almost sort of warm water thinking about my Tuesday class, Dr. Braddock's Narratives of the American West, to the presentation I had to give:::::::::::::::*Into the Wild*, I could nail that, knew that story from my heart, had lived it, had been a romantic refugee all my life, a concept hard for civilians and other losers to understand:::::::::::::when I dressed—clean clothes, cleaner, at least—and came out, Barnes was in bed watching *All My Children*: it was just starting—

"You're really going to school?" Barnes.

"Sure." Me. "I have to make a presentation."

"Fuck!" Barnes laughed—*ha-ha!*—and the hounds looked at him, delighted. "You're going to make a presentation? In class? Today?"

"Sure—"

"Oh, Travis—oh, my young and inexperienced friend! You've got to learn to transcend that bullshit!"

"Hey, I'm transcending." Really: Dr. Braddock's class was probably the only class I was going to pass this semester, certainly the only class I cared about—not that I even gave the slightest shit about the other classes::::::::::::::I basically wasn't even going any more, fuck them—

The commercial ended and *All My Children* came back on: Tad was talking to Jesse about Dixie's murder—poor Dixie: Barnes had liked her a lot. He had been watching *All My Children* since he was in high school, in the early 70s, and he was far more attached to the characters in the show than he was to any living people, to anyone except the hounds, and he'd gotten me addicted to it, too. Luddie the hound jumped down off the bed, then hopped up onto the couch, next to me: the hounds always watched AMC with us.

"You know these people I go to class with." Me. "They're a bunch of losers, they're a bunch of civilians, they're scared of everything—they'd die if they tried to do what I do!"

"News for you, kid." Barnes. "Most people don't want to do what you do."

"Kendall needs to forget about being friends with

Bianca." Me. I was looking at the show. A commercial came on, and I went to my bedroom and packed up my stuff: phone, *Into the Wild*, Edward Abbey's *Desert Solitaire*, a notebook. Stuck it all in a black messenger bag, then laid out another line of crank and sucked it up::::::::::::::::::::::::::

Out front, Barnes was already dozing, and he had his teeth out, looking old. Luddie thumped her tail on the couch and I sat next to her and put on my sneakers. On the television, Kendall and Bianca were talking again:::::::::::::::::::really, everything around me was soap opera—my life was a soap opera—yes, *I* was a soap opera——

:::::

About class: it was a lot of work, readings and papers and presentations, and I don't know why I hung in there with it, I suppose maybe only because I liked it—liked the subject: the west, narrative, stories. I'd been west a couple of times, to Yellowstone and Colorado, and I liked stories, and I thought the trips were stories, that I was *in* a story, that I *was* a story. Dr. Braddock knew that, I think: could see that I cared, even though I was kind of a fuckup—the kind of fuckup who didn't really care too much about being a fuckup....

And so I was still cranking a little when I got to Calhoun Hall—cranking jangling sagging buzzing—tired from my night in jail—but still ready to talk about the book I'd read. We were meeting in a dim room, in a sort of half-basement, some spring light filtering in and down. I had a special seat near the end of the long seminar table, a seat on Dr. Braddock's right, where I could look at her clearly, watch her, then turn to the screen if I needed to and look at the slides. It was my special place: earlier in the semester this kid named Jared sat in it, and I told him to move—told him that I needed to sit there, and he moved. He went around the table and took a chair on Dr. Braddock's left, about midway on the table, and from where I sat I could look down at him—from my seat, my special place. Jared was presenting, too, *Desert Solitaire*, a book I knew was beyond his ken, a book that I knew was opposed to the values of his whole life. Other people in the class were a usual assortment of students: frat guys in flip-flops, an artsy girl all in black, neatly dressed boring sorority girls. The only people I paid attention to were Jared, my enemy, and Nelda Krueger, who'd been in my fall semester Writing and Rhetoric class—a semi-boring girl, but with potential.

Dr. Braddock came in carrying the Krakauer book and the Abbey book, a clipboard and a legal pad. No laptop, so apparently we weren't going to look at slides, just have presentations and discussions. Very good: I wanted to hear what that asshole Jared had to say, and then I wanted to *step* on him::::::::::::::::::::::::I'd just gotten out of jail! I was a crazyman! I was dangerous! On drugs! He needed to be afraid of me—!

"So." Dr. Braddock. "Let's get started. Does anyone have questions about the readings or about—anything?"

Nobody said anything or asked anything, people just rustled papers or notebooks or checked their cell phones that they were trying to keep hidden under the seminar table.

"All right." Dr. Braddock. "As you know, this is the last time we're meeting in this room—on Thursday, we're going to meet at my house, right? For an end-of-semester party." Dr. Braddock started passing around papers: a map out to her house went clockwise from her end of the table, and a sign-up list of what to bring went counter-clockwise. Both stacks of paper met at me, at the far end of the table, and I saw that I was still signed up to bring a bag of chips—about the only thing I could bring, really: most of the class was still underage, and so Wild Turkey was probably inappropriate—and crank, too. It wasn't a real party, anyway, just sitting around her house talking about books or whatever, but I really wanted to go.

"My house can be hard to find, so keep your eyes open." Dr. Braddock. "Also, your term papers are due Thursday, so bring them along with you."

"What if we can't come to the party?" Nelda.

"You can drop your paper off at the department office." Dr. Braddock. "They'll put a time stamp on it." Dr. Braddock didn't like late papers, didn't like electronic copies. She was old—but old with principles, a purist. She didn't like what she didn't like. "Take the papers seriously, but don't stress about them. I'd like these last meetings to be a celebration of what we've achieved this semester."

Poor Dr. Braddock: how much was achieved with these dullards and losers and idiots? Still, she tried:::::::::::::she tried, even if it was only me paying attention::::::::

"So, are there any questions about the party, or about the papers?" Dr. Braddock. No one said anything, people just looked at their notebooks or phones. "Okay, so let's start with the presentations. Jared, you read *Desert Solitaire* for us, correct?"

"Yeah." Jared. Fucking Jared in his little ironed oxford shirt, his hip glasses, his stupid hair slicked up into a little peak right at the top of his forehead—he frowned, looked at his notes. "I didn't like this book much?" Fucking Jared, he talked like a girl, uptalking, raising his tone at the end of each sentence like he was asking a question. "It's about this guy, he gets a job as a park ranger? He spends a whole summer out in the desert?"

"That's what it's *about*?" Me. Almost shouting.

"Well, yeah?"

"It's about values—it's about—"

"Travis, you can ask questions later." Dr. Braddock. Okay, sure, slap my ass back into place. She said, "Go ahead, Jared."

Jared read the book, at least, I guess—but he didn't get it, no, not really. For Jared it was all about being impractical, about how civilization wins, has won, and everybody else, Ed Abbey and any other writer, any citizen who cares, needs to give it up and go out and buy a microwave oven or something. He believed in the manifest destiny of the corporation, the ultimate victory of the city, the car, and the highway—the economic monoculture—and everyone else, everyone who cared even a little bit about the world, could go off and die or at least shut up—including me::::::::::::::Jared, that piece of shit—

—Yet eventually he finished.

"It's about *morality*." Me. Again. "It's about trying to achieve some sort of—of—wholeness."

"Wholeness?" Jared.

"When he kills the rabbit?" Me. Now I was uptalking like fucking Jared.

"He kills a rabbit?" Nelda. Her big contribution to the discussion: looking sad and concerned about a fucking rabbit that died 50 years ago. What happens in the book is that Abby randomly pitches a rock at a rabbit crouching under a bush—and kills it. And leaves it for the vultures, for scavengers, leaves it with sort of a feeling of oneness with nature and the power of death.

"Doesn't mean anything to us now?" Jared. What? "We live in cities? Nature's over?"

"No—"

"You're a tree-hugger?"

Dr. Braddock was letting us argue, looking amused, looking pleased, looking like this was what she wanted.

"Hell, no!" Me. Hey, I like electricity, I like cars, I like air-conditioning—I even had a little window unit in my bedroom and could lounge comfortable and cool, while Barnes and the hounds were out scorching sweltering sweating in the front of the dilapidated unairconditioned bungalow. "But you know what? We should go blow up those dams, or let the terrorists come in and blow up the dams!"

People were looking at me like I was crazy, like I didn't know what I was talking about.

"It's like Tolstoy." Me. I'd taken a Tolstoy class: got a C in it, but I'd taken it, and I'd done the reading—I read *Anna Karenina*, I'd read *War and Peace*. As far as I was concerned, Tolstoy was so smart he trumped everything and everybody. I said, "Tolstoy—when he was old—was against sex, even though he knew that if sex was outlawed, the human race would go extinct."

All the other students laughed at me: and I suppose I kind of deserved it, because everyone is supposed to be in favor of sex even if they're not fucking very much or are churchily against it.

"So—we should just go ahead and blow up those dams." Me. Blushing—really.

Dr. Braddock wasn't laughing at me, though. "Destroy the village in order to save it?"

"Sure." Me. "Why not?"

"Well, it's not really very practical, is it? Even if we're not concerned with the continuation of the human race?"

"Well, no."

"So, as much as blowing the dams and killing off everyone might be desirable, it's not going to happen."

"Should!" Me. Not giving up.

"But won't. But think about this—what about the concept that wildness is an important part of the human condition? That we need nature?"

"You don't need nature to be—"

Dr. Braddock held up her hand. Shushed me—slapped my ass back into place again.

"We'll get back to you in a minute, Travis. What does anybody else think? Do we need wildness?"

Everybody in the room looked down—at the table, at the floor. Nelda, I saw, was looking at her lap—at her cell phone, probably.

"Anybody?"

Of course, Jared didn't have anything to say, and this was his presentation—or was supposed to be. Nobody had anything to say: *I* had things to say.

"Jenna?"

Jenna—the artsy girl. She flinched. "Well—I don't know. We went camping once—it was hot out. But if you want to go to the park, or something, that can be nice...."

Dr. Braddock sighed. I saw it. "Travis?"

"You don't need wilderness to be wild." Me—speaking very quickly in case she shushed me again. "All you need is the concept—"

"Which leads us into your presentation." Dr. Braddock, smiling at me. "*Into the Wild.*"

Okay: my turn: *Into the Wild.* I looked down at my notebook suddenly a little nervous, maybe confused. Not as jangly as I had been, though, for good or for ill. *Into the Wild,* by Jon Krakauer. Most of the people in the room had at least seen the movie, so I didn't have to describe the plot too much: Chris McCandless, this kid, goes wandering around the US, trying to find himself, looking; his asshole parents he cuts off out of his life and leaves behind; his trip to Alaska, his death. Actually, I guess I talked about the plot more than I should have, because Dr. Braddock stopped me.

"But why was he looking for his *self* in the wild?"

"He was wrong—he was mistaken." Me. Catching my breath. "You can find yourself in the city as easily as you can in the wilderness. Wild is everywhere. Maybe he just liked trees."

"I think it's horrible what he did to his parents." Nelda. "Not letting them know where he was."

"Aw, he should've dropped a fucking bomb on their heads!" Me. Several people looked shocked. I smacked the table with my hand. Bang! "A fucking bomb! He didn't owe them anything!"

Nelda looked at me. "His *life.*"

"He didn't ask to be born!"

"I don't know." Dr. Braddock. "I remember when I was an undergraduate, and I took off for a semester in Mexico, and I never told my parents. Can you believe that? All the time they thought I was safe in Northfield, and they were very scared and hurt when they found out I wasn't."

I wasn't going to diss her parents—not to her face, at least. But she didn't owe them anything, either. Not even her life. She should have dropped a big goddamn bomb on their heads.

"He could have at least given them a phone call." Nelda.

"That wouldn't have stopped him from dying?" Jared. Was he taking my side? Why?

"Looking out over the edge of a cliff doesn't mean anything if you're tied to a rope." Me. I thought about it. "Hunter Thompson says no one can talk honestly about the edge."

"Right." Dr. Braddock. "The only ones who even know where the edge is are the ones who've gone over it."

Dr. Braddock actually knew the quote, from *Hell's Angels*—I guess that's why she was a professor. She read a lot of books, all the books.

"Still." Me. "Calling home ruins everything."

"The wild would be just as wild." Dr. Braddock. "In the end, though, I'm not so interested in his parents. But what about all the people he met on his travels? All the people whose lives he touched—the old man, the people he worked with on the farm."

"They'd be just as touched even if he didn't die?" Jared.

"Maybe it took his death for them to realize they'd been touched." Me. "Or maybe they just made up being touched— maybe they're just a bunch of fucking liars."

"What does it say about human networks, though?" Dr. Braddock. "About how we're connected in life? Or *are* we connected in life? Is there some larger issue going on here?"

Nobody said anything—everybody looked at the floor, except Nelda, who looked at me.

"Isn't that pretty much what both these books are getting at?" Dr. Braddock. "The overall integration of wildness into the human experience?"

Everyone sort of nodded: if Dr. Braddock wanted us to take that from the books, we would, I guess. I was feeling drained—suddenly—and I didn't have much else to say, and class was about over, anyway. People began gathering up their books. Dr. Braddock stopped me just before I left the room.

"So, Travis—you seemed to be really personally involved in these books today."

"Sure." Me—blushing again. "Aren't we supposed to be?"

: : : : :

I slept most of the rest of the afternoon and on into the middle of the evening. Dark out when I woke up, and Barnes was not at home—off out getting drunk or shooting up, probably. I threw some food down for the hounds and then let them outside. I was hungry, too, and still tired—but I sat in my chair at my desk and looked at the computer: no emails, nothing on Facebook—my phone showed no missed calls—nobody was interested in me. I looked at the pile of books on my desk: I had to write a paper. Dr. Braddock's paper: something about the relationship between the photographer William Henry Jackson and painter Thomas Moran, and their trip to Yellowstone. Something. I had a biography of Jackson—and I had Dr. Braddock's book. Didn't have a paper, though. Wasn't going to write it tonight, either.

Outside, Baby-Killer was barking at something.

"Shut up!" Me. No paper tonight, no way. I got the crank out of my sock box and laid out a line. Now Luddie was baying too. I went to the back door and stuck my head out. "Hounds! Get back in here!"

Oh—a little crank was fine—no more lethargy::::::::Just a little jangle, not even enough to stop my appetite. I was hungry, and I needed to eat: the wonderful friendly cells of my body were asking, politely, for more than methamphetamine and beer. And, hey, I listened to my body.

"Okay!" Me. Aloud. I got to my feet and went to round up the hounds.

: : : : :

I found Barnes at the Chili Parlor, sitting at the bar with Crazy Larry.

"Oh! Yes! Here's my cellie!" Barnes. Smiling, craggy face all lit up. Pleased to see me. "I was telling Larry about our adventures in the prison-industrial complex."

"It was a triumph." Me.

"Being in jail?" Crazy Larry. He was a slender black man with frizzed-out hair, an orderly at the state hospital. "Yeah, jail's sure some triumph. I guess there's black people triumphing all the time in this town, huh?"

I ordered a beer and stepped aside to watch Barnes—he was leaning back on his barstool, rocking back and forth, rocking—

"—and so the turnkey comes up and starts banging on the cell door—he's yelling, 'You pieces a shit, you're the people who's been ruining this town!' and all, and I said, 'Yeah, motherfucker, I've been ruining this town for thirty years now, and I'm gonna keep on ruining it until you fucking *die!*"

"Yeah, you did, sort of." Me. "Kind of." Sort of kind of maybe not really but who cared.

"This is my fucking town!" Barnes. Stretching his arms out like he was being crucified, or maybe waving a helicopter in for a landing. "Fucking screws."

I was still jangled a little, a little::::but not too much, and hungry. I looked around and saw Dr. Broughton, a history professor I knew, sitting alone at a table by the front windows—alone, his wife had left him, or something, a few months earlier, and we would see him out and about all the time: if not at the Chili Parlor, then at the Tavern, or at the Little Wagon, drinking and watching basketball games, and I suppose unless he got a girlfriend or his wife came back, he'd soon be watching baseball in the bars, and then football—which is really not too bad a way to go through life, I thought. Broughton saw me looking at him, and he waved me over.

"So—you staying out of trouble?"

"Hell, no." Me. I sat down across from him. "I was in jail last night!"

"Oh, yeah?" Broughton. He looked like he was amused—he always seemed to think I was pretty funny. The class I'd had from him in the fall, The History of the Atomic Bomb, had been in the morning—late morning, 11:30, but morning all the same—and every class I'd made it to I'd had a hangover, or been half-loaded from staying up all night—and still I got an A.

"It was ridiculous!" Me. "It was crazy!"

"No doubt."

A waitress came by and I ordered a large Frito Pie with XX chili, and another beer and a glass of ice tea, too, and I told him the story: Barnes running the stop sign, the cops, the jail, people screaming all night, Barnes arguing with the turnkey—me laughing the whole time, and then the waitress brought me my chili and drinks, and I took a breath.

"And then—I gave a presentation this afternoon in my English class." Me. I smashed the chili into the corn chips.

"How'd you do?"

"I don't know. Good, I guess—I read the book, at least."

"That always helps." Broughton. "What about your other classes?"

"Oh, I sort of dropped them."

"Sort of?"

"I more or less stopped going." Me, eating. Eating. it was good. I was hungry! "I'll show up for the finals, take the tests."

"You're going to flunk out!" Broughton, laughing. "They'll ask for your financial aid back."

"Well, they can ask."

Broughton laughed again. Then he noticed the biography of William Henry Jackson I was lugging around—I brought it along with me thinking maybe I could make some notes at the bar, or something. "What's that thing for?"

"A paper." Me. I took a long drink of beer, and then of ice tea. "Paper about Jackson's photographs of Yellowstone. But I don't like my topic."

Broughton took the book and leafed through it, looking at all the pictures—Mount of the Holy Cross, View from Toroweap: old lost worlds almost forgotten, the West in black and white, caught forever, nothing now and gone.

"What's your topic?" Broughton.

"I don't really have one." Me. "That's why I don't like it."

"Ah." Broughton. He'd been teaching a long time: he'd had hundreds and hundreds of students over the years, thousands, and I suspect he'd heard this before, no doubt.

I tried to explain the paper to him—the idea for the paper: Jackson and Moran, great photographer, great painter, both on the 1871 Hayden Expedition to Yellowstone, the expedition that didn't exactly discover Yellowstone, but mapped it and made it known and resulted in the formation of Yellowstone National Park.

"So what?" Broughton. "That's what you have to answer—why is this important? What does it mean?"

"I don't know." Me. A lie: I did know—it was all in Chapter Seven of Dr. Braddock's book, how Jackson's and Moran's images helped shape what people think of when they think of the West—or, at least, of Yellowstone. When I started thinking about the paper, I thought she might like it that I'd read her book. Now I wasn't so sure, now I was afraid she might think I was a brown-nose suck-up, and I didn't want to tell anybody, and I didn't even want to write the paper anymore.

"Maybe I'll change my topic." Me.

"Change your topic to what?"

"I don't know—I'll come up with something."

"When's the paper due?" Broughton closed the book and looked up at me.

"Thursday." Me. "I'll come up with something."

"You're crazy!" Broughton. He laughed at me again. The waitress came around and he ordered more beers. "You'll never get it done."

"I like the pressure." Me. "I work well on the brink. I live on the edge."

Barnes came over and sat down heavily. When Broughton split up with his wife, Barnes kept bugging him to come by World of Pawn someday and hock his wedding ring, to turn his back on the past, to soak the ring and use the proceeds to do something useful, like get loaded.

"You're leading this kid into bad habits." Broughton. "Jail!"

"It's part of my educational process." Me.

"He's just a roommate." Barnes. "He pays his rent, he does

what he wants—we got no in loco parentis going on here."

"Loco's about right." Broughton. "The both of you."

Barnes was older than me, of course—older even than Broughton, I think—but it was fun for me and good for me to hang around with someone who had his shit together, even if he was a drug addict and a ne'er-do-well. A few days earlier I'd stopped by the condo where I'd lived before—my old roommates were there, walleyed college boys sitting around watching SportsCenter, listening to lame country music, dirty clothes rotting in piles until they could bag everything up and take it home for mommy to wash, old roommates Chad and Jerry looking at me kind of scared, clutching their iPhones to their chests, wary. I was jangled quite a bit that evening, velocitized, talking fast, sweating, trying to get them to move faster—go, go, go, go, go, go, go, go—trying to get going so we could get downtown and catch a band, the boys sitting in that big room, in that condo Chad's father had bought for him, sitting in the room with all their toys—skateboards, bicycles, computers, wii, wall-filling TVs—the room much neater and cleaner and tidier since I'd left, kicked out in all but name, my behavior so disturbing to them, so unnatural, so unnerving, that they recoiled, all those years of DARE propaganda they'd listened to in school kicking in—they sat there, idling when they should have been cruising, dawdling when they should have been bolting—and I knew—knew—that I was so, so fucking lucky to have my dark dank mildewy little room with the window unit in the dilapidated bungalow with Barnes and the hounds. I had a home!

Now Barnes and Broughton were arguing over World War II: Broughton wasn't a military historian, his specialty was the history of science, but if you're going to be a scholar of the atomic bomb and atomic science, you've got to know about Curtis Lemay and the XXI Bomber Command, and Barnes was a big Curtis Lemay fan—he was a big air force fan, period, and the front room of the ramshackle bungalow, the room shut off from the hounds, held his model airplane collection, an air armada he'd been working on for forty-odd years, little plastic and wood planes covering every surface in the room—his desk, his work table, hanging from wires dangling off the ceiling, stuck to the walls, photos of bomb damage from seven or eight wars. During one argument with Broughton, Barnes announced that he was going to spray the ramshackle bungalow for roaches on August 6, to commemorate the atomic bombing of Hiroshima, and he asked if that made him a racist. "Yeah, pretty much," Broughton said, and Barnes laughed and said something like how we all carried the fires of Armageddon in our hearts. Our fucking hearts! Incredible. He was a poet, too, and wild. Broughton was always amused by Barnes: just like he was amused with my craziness, he was amused with Barnes's obsessive antiquarianism—for Barnes was an antiquarian: it showed in the music he listened to and the drugs he took—he was like a Civil War reinactor who was so far into his stupid cult that he'd not only live on hardtack but try to own a slave or two, too: Barnes lived his obsessions. But Barnes was crazy, crazier than me, and crazier for a far longer time, and he could scare people with his starting startling green eyes and his loud voice and weird laugh: it was obvious that he was on something or had been on something or would soon be on something—his enthusiasms over borderline weirdnesses like atom bombs, college basketball, model airplanes, old rock'n'roll, motorcycles, LSD and heroin (a weird and volitile mix right there)—all crazy obsessive things! Fucked up on heroin or crank or vodka or acid, never never stopping talking talking ever ever—I remember bringing him by the condo once, before I was all but kicked out, Chad and Jerry cowering in fear, their girlfriends—the girls they hung out with, anyway, and maybe boned a time or two—also cringing back, while Barnes was in the bathroom pissing with the door open, pissing into the sink while he stared at his reflection in the mirror, like he was hypnotizing himself with his massive flopping uncircumcised dick dangling out, pissing on and on and on and on and on and on and on and on.... "Don't bring him around here again," Chad whispered after a while. "I live here, too," I said, but I didn't for much longer.

Broughton was a serious guy, an tenured academic at a big university, and though he was drunk and depressed a lot of the time, maybe most of the time, he had a sense of humor: he could see the point of Barnes and Barnes's project—his life—which was maybe similar to the project I was working on, too: an anachronistic, antiquarian, fucking nuts project.

"See, it was the B-29B model that was specially configured for Lemay's firebomb attacks." Barnes. "Get rid of the 50-cals and those babies could carry more ordinance, burn more cities, lay more waste, bring more American culture to the world."

"That's all in the Michael Sherry book." Broughton. "The Rhodes book too—and elsewhere."

"Sherry is better on the development of the theory of aerial warfare—"

"Guilio Douhet!" Me. Hey, I got an A in that class.

"Rhodes and Sherry both spend too much time on the implications of the Bomb." Barnes. He'd been a grad student in American Studies at one time: a semester and a half in 1979 or so, before he got busy being drunk and drugged and crazy. "All I want is information about the hardware."

"C'mon, you know the implications are what's important." Broughton. "The hardware's just the romantic part."

"Huh?" Me. "If you can romanticize the atomic bomb...."

But I thought: I'm a romantic, though, and I'm a bomb.

An atom bomb, even. Right?

"All the implications—the rise of the national security state, big government, big industry, big science, big universities—"

"And big science in the big universities!" Barnes. "Ha! They're all squeezing out the humanities—you're doomed!"

"Not science so much." Broughton. "Big business is the real enemy, the way they're bringing your fucked-up consumer ethos into the classroom—they want to turn us into goddamn shopkeepers. Pawnbrokers."

"That's called progress." Barnes. "This used to be a college town—now it's, I don't know, just some big fucking thing."

"Oh, don't start crying about old Austin." Me. Really, it was boring listening to old people whine about the fucking golden days when they were young and everything was fun. Right now was fun, too. And tomorrow would be even funner.

"No, it was different." Barnes. "Broughton knows this. Like, the university used to let people come in and run on the track—now they moved the track out of the stadium to a new place, and they put a fucking fence around it."

"Yeah, I bet you ran on the track a lot." Me.

"Chasing smack dealers and hookers, maybe." Broughton. "But, yeah, you're right—the university's separated itself from the community, built a fence. That's the corporation talking. Everything's about money now. Shit, they even kicked the state historical association off campus."

"Who the hell cares about Texas history?" Barnes.

"Me?" Me. I sort of cared, maybe.

"Not the university." Broughton. "It doesn't turn a profit."

"Okay." Me. It was like I was caught in a crossfire: Barnes hated the university because he hadn't made a life there, and Broughton hated the university because he had. "But what difference does it make for a student? So what if some fucking bum can't come in and run laps on the track?"

"The corporation's going to give you larger class sections, more online classes, less-qualified teachers." Broughton. "You might notice, maybe not. Most kids are only here for four years, not long enough to see a difference."

"Students are stupid." Barnes.

"Hey!" Me. Though I suppose he was right about everyone else besides me.

"Ignorant's probably a better word." Broughton. "Maybe innocent. Students don't really know what professors do, or what the university does."

"Which is your own fucking fault." Barnes. "You're all up in that ivory tower, whacking off—"

"You." Broughton pointed across the table at me. "You're going to be one of the last people to get a real education here, before they break up the university and really turn it into a business."

"Education's overrated." Barnes. He had a depraved hard laugh, like a parrot: *ha-ha!* "Who needs an education when you can get the History Channel on basic cable?"

"The Military Channel." Me.

"The fucking Military Channel! Or the fucking Pentagon Channel!" On days off, Barnes would usually spend all day with the hounds watching *The World's Deadliest Aircraft* or whatever for hours and hours, occasionally getting out of bed to shoot up or roll a joint. "Somebody needs to drop a bomb on the college, get you parasites out doing useful work, like plumbing or fixing cars."

Barnes was always mad at the university. I sat back against the window and looked over at the bar to see if there was anyone else hanging around that I knew—but nobody interesting had come in. A week earlier at closing time a woman saw me standing around and offered me a ride home—we'd been talking a bit earlier, about something weird, I suppose, but I was barely paying attention to her, and then she thought I needed a ride. My car was parked right across the street, but I said Sure, and I got in her car and she reached over and started adjusting my willie before we even got around the block to Guadalupe—but she didn't want to go inside the dilapidated bungalow when we got home: the hounds were at the front door, howling and jumping around, scratching at the screen, and she was afraid.

"Those are some big dogs...."

"Hounds." Me. "They're sweethearts!"

"They're scary."

So we fucked right there, on the front seat of her car, a tangle of jeans and underwear and banging into the damn steering wheel, Baby-Killer and Luddie baying inside the house, and I looked down once and the woman was looking laughing up at me with crazy cheerful eyes—but then there was a flash of light and it was Barnes getting back.

"Oh, ho!" Barnes. Standing outside the car with his weird

parrot laugh, and the hounds were suddenly surging and leaping around and we finished and I got out and the woman drove away and Barnes stood there laughing at me. "Travis, you are a dog!"

"Aw." Me. A little breathless. "Yeah...."

"You guys should have at least crawled into the back seat!"

"Too much trouble."

Inside Barnes was going through his record collection, his thousands and thousands of old vinyl albums. His speakers and his turntable were new and top quality—he was a pawnbroker, after all—but the amplifier and the records were ancient, antiques, Barnes the antiquarian—the amp actually was actually 20 or so years older than I was, and it ran on tubes, vacuum tubes, and it got hot when it played, got hot and glowed. Barnes dropped side one of *Exile on Main Street* onto the turntable and cranked the volume, and the rest of the set list was lined up, nothing newer than 25 years old: Clash, Buzzcocks, Stranglers, Paul Revere and the Raiders— all old rock'n'roll, oldish at least—Joan Jett, Jackson Five, Husker Du—and I got mugs of vodka from the kitchen and a package of speed from the bedroom, and the tubes glowed and the records played and the hounds jumped around and Barnes jumped around and I jumped around—and this, really, I thought, this is what life should be like all the time: booze, drugs, fucking, rock'n'roll, jumping around all night for no good reason—forever—forever——

But now the waitress came with more beers, and Barnes ordered a round of shots, some sort of awful ginger brandy that no one else drank except when he was buying, and Crazy Larry came over and sat with us, and some other people, and Broughton finally got up to leave and he squeezed me on the shoulder as he left and he said, "Good luck with the paper." The paper: I hadn't thought about it in hours, it seemed like, even though the biography of Jackson was still there on the table—Larry was looking through the photographs—and I didn't want to think about it, and didn't want to write it, either: it was a stupid topic.

"So—what do you think?" Me, looking at Larry. "Is that interesting at all?"

"Those people were doing some hard travelling back in those days." Larry. "They didn't have roads or trucks or anything to haul that shit around."

"Jackson was a bull-whacker." Me. About the only thing I could remember from the book, and that was only because it sounded like he was masturbating and not driving an ox-cart. "But, yeah—those cameras were huge—they had tons of shit to pack around."

Then the lights went up in the bar: closing time. We straggled out into the night, Barnes and Larry and myself, and the other drunks, into the cool night, the capitol dome pale white rising above us, all the streetlights reflecting up into the sky, cars heading back to the university—closing time all over town, drunks and crazy people heading home. I took a deep breath: tired, tired, now, but I had work to do.

: : : : :

How about:

> Travelling into the Yellowstone Country was a
> hard task—up into the wilderness with spouting
> geysers and misting steams and hauling tons
> of equipment slung on packhorses and mules
> and wagons groaning and scared of Indian
> attacks and the unknown of hell and with the
> moron Ferdinand V. Hayden leading the way to
> discovering what was there. Except other people
> were already there, setting up hotels at the
> healthy hot springs to make money off tourists—
> so it wasn't really a wilderness at all....

No! Who wanted to read 12 pages of that shit? Not even me. I needed some sleep, and I crawled into bed and shut out the light.

: : : :

In the morning it didn't get any better.

> Riding up into the mountains, draggle-
> slagging and bull-whacking behind their
> stupid retarded leader, Thomas Moran and
> Wm Henry Jackson didn't know that they
> were on their way to demonstrating a new
> understanding of American nature. And
> their idiot leader—Ferdinand V. Hayden—
> leading them further and further away from
> what might be called civilization into the
> garish crazy bubbling labyrinth of time and
> mountains that would one day be called
> Yellowstone….

And—no. No! Three more hours of sleep. Or five.

: : : : :

Dr. Holt's office was down in the basement of the undergraduate library, in a big wide room with a low ceiling whose tiles were all half-broken and stained with urine or whatever was flowing down from upstairs—a crowded room, a sad room where you expected to see cancer-riddled mutants with red glowing eyes sitting in the shadows grading papers. Holt was sitting slumped at his desk, staring straight ahead at a leaking sewer pipe.

"Hey, Dr. Holt."

He jerked around. "What?" He looked at me. Peered at me. "Huh?"

"Remember me? I was in your—" Fuck me, I couldn't remember the course number. "Your, uh, class last fall."

"Yeah." Holt. He kept looking at me, not like he was scared, or pissed, but like he didn't know who I was or what I wanted, or why I wanted anything—a tired watery stare, and then he looked past me at the cubicle wall, and I turned and looked, too, but all I could see was a poster for an old movie, *The Paper Chase*. Holt looked at me again, and sighed, and sank back into his chair. He said, "It's too late to complain about your grade."

"What?" Me. "I got an A!"

"You did?"

"Yeah!"

"Well." Holt slouched down some more.

"I just wanted to talk to you a minute." Me, smiling. "Are you busy?"

Holt opened his mouth, then shut it. Just then Profesora Jennifer, his officemate, came pushing by me into the cubicle. I smiled at her, too: she'd been my teacher for second semester Spanish.

"Hola, Profesora!"

She looked at me. "Hey, Señor Travis! Como esta?"

"Uh—pretty good." Me. "I forget—"

"C'mon, you need to practice! ¡Hablame en español!"

I smiled at her. "Uh...."

"Travis! How are you going to speak to people when you visit Mexico?"

"I'll take you with me?" Of course, I'd probably end up in jail for real if I ever went to Mexico. And a Mexican jail was probably less fun than the drunk tank in Austin. "You can be my translator!"

"Ha!" Profesora Jennifer was a lot of fun.

"You wanted to speak with me?" Holt. Now he was looking kind of pissed.

"Yeah, if that's okay."

"Let's go outside." Holt got up and squeezed past me out of the cubicle, and I waved goodbye to Profesora Jennifer, and I followed him back through the dingy low-ceilinged room and out to the patio, bright sunshine and breeze. We sat at a big table shaded by an umbrella.

"So—is there some problem?"

"Aw, no." Me. "Not a problem. I just kind of wanted some advice—about a paper."

"A paper." Holt was staring at me again. "A paper we did last semester?"

"No, a paper I'm writing *this* semester—for a different class, for a class I'm taking this semester."

"I've got—" Holt sagged again. Stared past me. "I've got, like, 180 students."

I thought: Well, one more won't hurt. Then I remembered what Broughton had been saying, how the corporatists—the edu-capitalists!—were ruining my education. And now here was the proof: poor Dr. Holt and his over-numbered sad 180 students.

"That's too many." Me.

"Yeah—"

"I know this history professor, Pete Broughton? He was telling me that the humanities are getting totally screwed over—classes are too big, you don't get paid enough—"

"Yeah, no kidding."

"So." Me. I was trying to think fast. Some crank would have helped. "So, I don't know—maybe here's your chance to fight back, right? Subvert the corporation. Do your job—educate."

He laughed at that. "Oh, come on."

"You're a professor, right? Profess me."

"I'm not a professor. I'm a lecturer. I'm a nobody."

"Same difference." I was pretty it was the same difference. They were all teachers of some sort. "It's still your job, right? What happens here changes the fucking world."

He didn't say anything, though—didn't even look at me. I sat there waiting for a bit. Barnes always told me to go ahead and ask people for things—they can always say no.

"It's for Dr. Braddock's class." Me. "I just wanted to run some ideas past you. It's no big deal."

Holt looked like he was in pain.

"You always said to talk though our essays when we got stuck." Me. "So—I'm really stuck."

"Have you talked to—to—Dr. Braddock about it?"

"Naw, her office hours—you know, I can't come in then." They were in the fucking morning. Obviously, I couldn't come in then. "But she wrote on my proposal." I pulled out everything from my messenger bag, all my paper junk—the stupid Jackson biography, Dr. Braddock's book, William Goetzmann's *West of the Imagination*, my notebook, a folder with a bunch of papers. I pulled the proposal from the folder—looked at it—then pushed it across the table to Holt.

"'Look to my book's works cited for some sources.'" Holt, reading. "So, she wants you to write something original."

"Yeah." Me. That was the problem—originality. She already wrote the fucking book. "But, you know, I really don't like this topic."

"Then why write it?"

Fucking Holt. Sitting across the table from me: it was easy for him: no pressure at all, no paper due the next day, no other classes to be maybe failed, no tiredness, weariness, weirdness—nothing looming over him, no nothing—

Holt took the Goetzmann book and began looking through it. "So, why'd you want to write about this, anyway?"

"I thought maybe she'd like it if I read her book?"

"She'd like it better if you could just write a good paper." Holt. He wasn't even looking at me, he was looking at pictures in the book. From where I sat it looked like a Remington painting.

"Yeah?" Me.

"About something you care about."

Well, shit. What did I fucking care about? That was the whole problem—with everything, really, with my whole goddamn life—what I cared about. I started college as a journalism major, then switched to history because journalists were stupid, then switched again, to English, because I liked to read. Basically, all I wanted to do with my life was read books and bullshit about them and then fuck around at night and get loaded. What was the harm in that? I suddenly hated William Henry Jackson, I wanted to go back in time and bull-whack him, the piece of shit. His photographs were interesting, but so what.

"I really liked your class." Me. Suddenly depressed, feeling the paper deadline looming, the certainty of failure.

"You're about the only one." Holt. He was still looking at the book: a big photo of smiling prostitutes posing on a hilltop, with the San Francisco fire burning in the distance. "My evaluations sucked."

"Really? I got a lot out of that class."

"Well, you must have been absent the day I told people not to wait until the last minute to write their papers."

Ouch. Well, shit. I thought. Maybe I could show Dr. Braddock the page or two I'd tried to write, and she could give me an incomplete. The other classes I had—well, shit, there, too—but I could probably come in and take the finals and do fine, just based on the reading. Maybe. Sure I could—

"Don't worry about it too much." Holt. "Everybody writes their papers at the last minute."

"Of course."

"Nobody wants to admit that, though."

"Yeah?"

"Everything we say is a big lie."

I shrugged, looked at the Jackson book sitting out on the table top. There had to be a way I could get it done—it was only a 12-page paper, and even if I took two hours a page, I could get it done in time to take it to Dr. Braddock's. Plus, I already had two bad pages already written—and a works cited. So, I only had to write nine pages in under 24 hours. I could do that!

But I still had to figure out what I was going to write nine pages about.

Fuck you, William Henry Jackson.

"How much is nine divided by twenty-four?" Me.

"What?"

I could do it—I pulled out my phone and punched in some numbers. But the result didn't make any sense—0.375 or something. Then I tried dividing 24 by nine. Okay: a page every 2.6 hours. No problem. I looked at the Jackson book again: Fuck you, Wm. Ha—and there was my idea! I could write a paper about how much I hated Wm. Henry— and Thomas Moran, too, and I already hated and despised F.V. Hayden—how they were a blight on American history and the American landscape—how their role in preserving Yellowstone was an error, how the park should be blown up, mined—the idea of a national park, a wilderness preserve— was just a cruel fucking joke on unborn generations who would never know the true wilderness of Nature, anyway, but would still somehow have to find true wildness in their own souls—

"So." Holt. He put the Goetzmann book down, and sat there all pale with his thinning hair and tired tired watery eyes looking at me. Sitting up a little straighter now that I wasn't making him read anything. "What else have you been doing this semester?"

He didn't really want to know.

"Ah, not too much." Me. "I was in jail. I went to Big Bend for spring break. I was witness to a murder."

"Damn!"

The innocents. They never understood. I grabbed a pen and began writing:

> *Following the yellowstone river south upstream wandering witlessly into what is now the national park, the artsy fools WmHenry Jackson and Thomas Moran were sereiously fatally deluded*

Deluded into what? By what? By who? That idiot Hayden?

"Tell me about the murder." Holt. Sitting up now, and leaning forward across the table. Interested. "What happened?"

"You don't want to hear about that." Me.

"Actually, I don't want to hear about some stupid paper you're never going to finish."

: : : : :

And that, too. What to say about that? A night where a lot of things went wrong, especially for the dead guy, and one or two things went right. It was how we started the New Year, Barnes and myself—and the murderer—and how the dead guy ended it.

New Year's Eve: I didn't even know where we were. Barnes drove—I wasn't paying attention—to the party, at Podraza's, who worked at the same pawnshop chain as Barnes, World of Pawn: he was manager of Store #3, and he did well, was a short broad-shouldered guy with a fuzzy soul-patch under his lip, very intense. Podraza lived in some house, down some street, somewhere on the East Side, an old house, but it was fixed up nice, and of course like any pawnbroker, his house was full of stuff—lots of stuff, all kinds of stuff: anything interesting that comes up out of pawn, the manager will get in there first to buy it, and so they end up with every fucking conceivable power tool, gun, or electronic gizmo known to man. At Podraza's we went in through the garage, where we grabbed cups of beer from a keg, and the garage was stacked with top-of-the-line drills, sanders, chipping hammers, circular saws, jig saws—table saws, miters—enough goddamn tools to set up a construction—or destruction—business, and then we went into the living room, packed with people from all the World of Pawns, all dancing to Kanye West coming out of who knows how many speakers and three or four huge flat screen TVs all with some football game on—the Sugar Bowl, I think, fucking Oklahoma was playing, those assholes—and Christmas lights still sparkling twinkling flashing and the people all jumping around, writhing; Podraza's wife, Evie, a little square-shouldered woman with glasses and a big tattoo of a Cyclops on her left bicep, jumping around, too, and she yelled at us happily, and we went on through to the kitchen, where it was all a bit calmer, people making margaritas and talking, and I was getting a margarita to go with my beer when Podraza came by and grabbed me and Barnes and took us tramping up the stairs and down a hall to his gunroom—a room with a safe full of pistols and rifles and shotguns—and Podraza opened the safe and took out his newest shotgun, a Marlin Model 55 12-gauge goose gun with a huge long barrel.

"Fuck." Me. "You go goose hunting much?"

"Fuck no!" Podraza. He was just showing off. He put the shotgun back in the safe and then pulled out some powders and laid out some lines of what I thought was crank but later found out wasn't speed but sheba, sweet dreamy heroin, and we all did a line or two or three or four, and then I left Barnes and Podraza talking pawn gossip and I went tromping back down the stairs and through the dancing pawnbrokers—T. Pain playing now—and back out to the kitchen and the margaritas—the blender whirring and the bass in the front room thumping and people yelling: a true Gatsby party. I wasn't jangled or velocitized, just dreamily vague from the sheba, sort of taking it all in, absorbing the world. In the kitchen was this old hippie musician, Zollie, who worked at Store #7 with Barnes, and he was rocking back on his heels and saying "Aw, damn," every few minutes very cheerfully, though he was also keeping an eye on his wife, a retired stripper named Honey, who was wandering around with her boobs half hanging out and her belly piercing glittering, Zollie smoking a joint and hitting the tequila pretty good. There were three Vietnamese sisters in the kitchen, all of them pawnbrokers at one World of Pawn or another, and I was talking to one of them, Vanessa, part-time pawnbroker and full-time student, and I think she kind of liked me.

"I'm an outlaw!" Me. "Give me a situation—*any* situation—I'll brink it."

"Sounds dangerous!" Vanessa, laughing.

"I defy the laws of man and god, I defy gravity—I defy common sense! I ain't nothing but a rebel!"

"Should I be scared?"

"No—of course not—I work only for the forces of good!"

"Yeah?"

"Yeah!"

Everyone was yelling over the music from the front—Jay Z, then old Prince—people dancing now in the kitchen, Honey saying something sharp to Zollie—yeah, I was looking at her boobs, too—a scattering of brown freckles across the top of her chest, flecks of gold and green glittering plastic mylar in her hair. A New Year coming, ready to unspool like a spool of Kevlar thread, and I was ready to unspool, too—no doubt a good year was coming, nothing but good news for everyone—

Then somebody counted down and—bang!—it was a New Year and people were cheering in the front room and there were tequila shots going around and I kissed Vanessa and one of her sisters, the girls tasting like salt and lime, and then Barnes was there.

"Time to go—"

"What? No!"

"We'll be back—we'll be back—we'll be back." Barnes—babbling, eyes glowing. "We'll be back. We just need to run out and play the first pool game of the New Year—we've got to celebrate, mark the occasion, play a little stick—"

And that made sense. Mark the occasion.

I looked at Vanessa. "Come with us—?—"

"Pool?" Vanessa, as if that was a very strange idea. She looked at her sisters. I could feel the vibrations of the house—everything throbbing, booming—

"Yeah!" Me.

"You're crazy!" Vanessa.

"Yeah!" Me. Then Barnes was dragging me out the back door. "Wait for me!"

: : : : :

So, now, sitting on the patio in the bright spring sunshine with grackles hopping and fluttering around—one big grackle pecking angrily at an empty Styrofoam cup—now, sitting with Holt, and he was looking at me.

"So, the murder was at the party?"

"No, no." Me. "We were at the party—it was New Year's,

and then we went out, and then things happened."

"Long story." Holt.

What the fuck. "You're the one who wanted to hear it."

"Well, yeah—"

: : : : :

We ended up at a bar called the El Caníbal Feliz. It's over on a side street off of East Sixth—not the nightclub district East Sixth where all the kiddie drunks go, but east East Sixth, way east of the interstate, on the far East Side, where all the brown and black people live, or used to live before gentrification, before all the rich white people kicked them out. El Caníbal Feliz—I hadn't been there before, had never heard of it, didn't even know where it was until a few days later when I went driving around to see what had happened, wherever whatever happened, and I found it sort of half-hidden behind some yaupon holly. But that night was New Year's and Barnes was driving, the great wheelman, and the night was cloudy and damp and cool, with sometimes a little bit of wind, and there were little flashes of light in the sky, fireworks going off, and cheerful little pops from rockets or people shooting guns in the air, you know—celebrating the changing year.

Then the car skidded to a stop and I braced myself against the dashboard.

"El Caníbal Feliz!" Barnes. "The Happy Cannibal—this sounds promising!"

And there it was: a red neon sign that said BEER. Below that a white sign, a handmade wooden sign with a light shining on it that said "El Caníbal Feliz" with a drawing of little skeleton reclining in a hammock slung between two palm trees. And so out of the car and across the street and into the bar all warm and smoky—and everything inside didn't quite come to a stop, didn't quite come to a standstill, everyone turning and looking at us, not quite—but it was close. Felt close. People noticed us, for sure: Barnes and myself were the only Anglos in the room. Everyone else was Mexican, mostly male—I could see a very few women off at tables near the walls—the bar crowded and smoking with Spanish music that sounded cheerful and sad at the same time, though my Spanish was too lousy to pick up on the words being sung.

Barnes put quarters down on the edge of one of the two pool tables, the one furthest from the bar, and there were already four quarters ahead of us from people waiting to play, and I went up to the bar—it was busy there, too, the bartender an intense younger guy with slicked-back hair, and I eventually got his attention and ordered eight Budweisers. When I got back to the table with the beers, Barnes was waiting leaning against the wall.

"Here we are, Travis." Barnes. "The New America. Se habla espanol."

"Yeah." Me. "It's pretty cool."

"Ninety percent of these people will be in the pawn shop at some point." Barnes gestured, waved his arm at the people, at the whole bar. "They'll be coming in pawning their screwdrivers, their lunchboxes—fifty cents here, a dollar there. We'll exploit them, turn our profit, and then somebody else will exploit us."

"Sure." Me. The true never-ending code of the pawn shop. "Big fish eat the little fish."

Barnes handed one of our beers to a short Mexican man standing against the wall. "Have you met our friend, Carlos?"

"Hey." Me.

"Yeah," Carlos said. "I'm feeling good!" Carlos stuck out his hand and I shook it.

"Muy barocho, eh?" Me.

Carlos nodded, stood listing in the smoky bar.

"I think I'm going to offer him a job at World of Pawn." Barnes.

Why not? Made sense to me. As much sense as anything else. World of Pawn always needed Spanish-speaking clerks. Then it was our time to play pool, and Barnes racked and I broke, and Barnes beat me. Then I racked and he broke, and he beat me again. My game was off, my brain was off—I wasn't jangled but dreamy: the New Year was only an hour or so old, and things were already going wrong. I've always heard that whatever you do on the first day of the year, you do for the rest of the year, and I was losing. Not a good sign, not at all, and I thought of Vanessa—how she tasted of the New Year, salty and warm—a much more pleasant thought.

"Let's go back to the party." Me.

"What's wrong with you?" Barnes. "We just got here—go buy more beers and maybe I'll let you beat me."

So I crossed the room, music playing, smoke in the air. When I got to the bar, I found a youngish-looking black man sitting there, a kid, really, a kid about my age, sitting there on a stool—very odd that was, odder and more out-of-place even than the Anglo-ness of Barnes and myself—but I didn't really think anything about him, he was just there, drinking a beer. I noted his presence, his youngishness, his oddness, but I didn't really think about it, I just stepped up to the bar to buy more beers, I tried to get the bartender's attention, and then I heard someone say "nigger."

Yeah, I noticed that.

I turned to look, and as I did, the black kid bumped into me, a soft bump. I stepped back a bit, staggered back into whoever was behind me. People were clearing out of the way—something was going on—a Mexican in a dark jacket was moving forward—a punch or something, and a noise, a ripping sound, something, something—I don't know what it was. Ripping. The kid leaning into me, kind of heavy, the Mexican in the dark jacket coming at him. I had a twenty dollar bill in my hand to pay for the beers—I remember that. I somehow slid around the kid and stood there like an idiot and said, "Hey—hold it."

Hey—hold it.

What the fuck was I doing?

Listen, I can still see that fist coming at me—coming out of the darkness, I can count the knuckles on it. I know, that sounds stupid, like a cliché, but its true—I can still see it. That fist coming straight at my face and them—blam! Bang! Ka-boom ka-pow! Impact—holy shit, and I went reeling back from the bar—stumbling staggering backwards, until I hit a table and fell across it, and then the table collapsed sideways, bottles and pitchers of beer showering down on me, falling with me, and I thought—whoa, this is just like a movie. Another total cliché, but that's what I thought.

: : : :

"But I think I remember you saying in class that clichés were clichés because they were true." Me. "Or something. Right?"

"What the hell." Holt.

"But you did say that, right?"

"Maybe—yeah, probably. But what happened? What started the fight?"

"Fuck if I know." Me. "I was just standing there at the bar, and I heard somebody call this black kid the n-word."

"Jesus."

: : : :

I don't think I was knocked out. There was a gap after the clichés, after hitting the table, a gap, and then I heard Barnes yelling, "He's down! He's down! He's limp!" Me, limp. But I somehow got up, all drenched with spilled beer and cigarette ashes, stumbling up. Staggering. I saw that the bar was almost vacant—almost empty, everybody gone running away, everyone gone but the bartender with his slicked-back hair, and the black kid, and drunk Carlos—and Barnes, and me. The kid was hunched over holding his belly, swaying a bit, Barnes with a hand on his shoulder, peering into his face. Carlos kept saying, "Oh, man."

Barnes. "Call 911."

The bartender said something like—He don't need 911, he's fine.

"Call 911!"

The kid tried sitting on a barstool. First he felt around for it with one hand, then he tried sliding up and on.

The bartender said, He's fine.

Then the kid fell off the barstool and hit the floor—thud.

Oh, man.

He's fine!

Barnes bent over him and then straightened up, stood up, his arms covered up to his elbows in blood.

The bartender bolted—I don't know where he went.

Barnes took my jacket off—I took it off and gave it to him, I don't remember but I guess he asked for it—took my jacket, and wrapped the wounded kid in it. I thought, I have a cell phone. I do remember thinking that, so maybe I was coming out of being punch-drunk—I have a cell phone. So I punched in the keys for 911, told them we needed the cops, needed an ambulance. But where? I didn't even know where the fuck we were. Some bar down some street somewhere. The Cannibal Club, I remembered. El Caníbal Feliz! Barnes yelled. The Happy Cannibal! Seventh Street! Or Sixth Street! So that's what I said—the Happy Cannibal! Seventh! Sixth! Somewhere. Somewhere! Barnes was doing mouth-to-mouth on the bleeding kid—I watched him and wondered if you're really supposed to do that for someone who'd been stabbed, I wondered if that might pump all his blood out. I didn't know—I don't know. I just stood there with Carlos watching. Then an ambulance pulled up and the medics came running in, and then the cops. The medics tossed my jacket in the corner and I got it and put it on, all bloody and dripping, I didn't even think about it. Barnes was telling a big fat white cop, "We saw what happened!" I said, "Yeah, we saw what happened!"

But the cop said—Yeah, we know what happened, the guy got stabbed.

We saw it!

We saw it!

You guys need to get the fuck out.

And so the cop pushed us—just pushed us—to the back door and through it and out into the alley, and the door shut.

And so that was really about it, what happened. We were out in the alley, and Carlos was crying now, and Barnes was crying—Barnes! Crying!—and I was standing there with my cell in my hand, dripping blood and gore from my jacket, cold, and all of a sudden I remembered that twenty dollar bill I'd had in my hand. Where'd that go? What happened to my twenty dollars?

That's all I cared about. I just wanted my twenty fucking dollars.

:::::

"So, basically, I suck." Me.

"The cops didn't take your names?"

"What?" Was Holt listening? "Fuck no."

"But you were witnesses!"

"Cops don't care." Me. I couldn't look at Holt. I looked past him, down the courtyard to an ATM machine: some kid punching numbers into the machine, taking money. I didn't want to talk any more—I'd talked too much. Of course more shit happened: we went back to the party, told the story to Podraza and everybody, then went out to breakfast all bloody, then to the cop station to make them listen, the fucking idiots, and they eventually caught the murderer. But there was no reason to tell Holt—or anyone. We sat quietly for a while.

"Okay." Holt, finally. "So, okay, tell me something—why are you wasting your time trying to write this piece of shit paper when you have a real story to tell?"

He pushed the William Henry Jackson proposal across the table to me.

I didn't say anything.

:::::

Okay. How about:

People die all the time, I know, though they
usually don't die wrapped up in my jacket,
blood and gore and guts soaking through
and dripping splatting everywhere. But this
is a violent world, just like the old West.
Except in a western, they usually shoot
each other, not stab each other, and I'm not
in most westerns.

No. How about:

I always thought I lived in a book, until it
turned out I lived in a movie—a violent
one, where bombs go off and people roll
around screaming and dying and

No, not really.

: : : : :

In the evening I met up with Barnes at the Tavern, after
he got off work, and we sat at the bar under the black-and-
white photos of long-gone bartenders, artifacts from a past
where everyone looked like they were having a grand time in
that golden age Barnes and the other olds would talk about,
those people in the pictures I never knew from a world I
couldn't even feel, really—while all around us living people
were bustling around and having at least some little bit of
fun—Happy Hour.

"No no no no no no no no no no—no." Barnes. "No! This
is not a story you want to write down."

"Sure it is." I was pretty sure, now.

"Some little black guy drawing his last breath in a puddle
of blood on a concrete bar floor. Bunch of Mexicans running
for the door. Two stupid white guys who don't know enough
to mind their own fucking business."

"We were heroes!"

"Heroes are stupid." Barnes. "You got punched in the nose by a murderer. That's pretty fucking stupid, if you ask me."

The cops had thought so, too. How come he didn't stab you? One of the detectives asked me that, and I didn't know. The murdered punched me, he didn't stab me. He just didn't. I just stood there and got punched, got knocked on my ass, and I didn't ask why.

"Now you're blaming the victim." Me.

"And how is this a narrative about the American West?"

"I don't know." Me. "We're in the west, I guess, and I'll write it as a narrative. I'll figure it out."

Actually, I had an idea: how many people die violently in western narratives? Lots of them: people dying everywhere—*Lonesome Dove, No Country for Old Men, The Grapes of Wrath, Sometimes a Great Notion, High Noon, Shane, The Wild Bunch*...just about every western story had a body count—people dying everywhere, often violently. Boot Hill was always full. And how many people got a chance to be in an actual no-shit violent western narrative? Not many—I was the only one I knew. There were other people at the bar that night, sure, but none of them were going to tell the story, or at least tell it like I might be able to tell it. Dr. Holt gave the idea, an outline: compare the murder to a book or movie and then explain what it means—to me. Put it in context, look for meaning, and so forth, like the teachers always wanted you—wanted me—to do. Of course, now I had to figure out what it meant and I had to figure out how to write it.

"Better get busy figuring if you're gonna get it done." Barnes.

"Oh, I'll pull it off." Me.

"Yeah, good luck with that."

We were sitting at the bar and I could see past Barnes to the door, and I looked up and saw Nelda Krueger come in with some other girls.

"Stop drooling." Barnes. He didn't even turn to see who I was looking at.

"What?" Me. "Fuck you."

The girls were looking for a place to sit in the crowded

bar, looking. I slid off my barstool and went over.

"Hey." Me.

"Oh—" Nelda looked surprised, though we ran into each other pretty often around town, Nelda always with a pack of girls who sort of looked alike, flat blond hair and blue or brown eyes, basic ordinary everyday white girls. Nelda was a bit darker. "What're you doing here?"

"Drinking." Me. "It's Happy Hour!"

"There's a table." A blond girl pointed. "By the window."

They started working their way toward the empty table. I grabbed my mug of beer—Barnes was already intently talking to some guy next to him—and followed the girls over.

"Still working on your paper?" Me.

"Oh, I finished." Nelda.

"No shit?" Me. Nelda finishing a paper early. How'd that happen? "What'd you write about?"

"Uh, *A River Runs Through It.*"

"Yeah? You liked that?"

"Brad Pitt was in the movie." Nelda. A waitress came over and took orders from the girls, then took some time looking at their fake IDs before heading to the bar to get the drinks.

"He gets killed at the end." Me. The character, Paul, gets killed in the book, too—really, the whole book is about dealing with the aftermath of violence. I thought about that.

"I guess I sort of wrote about environmentalism, stuff like that." Nelda. "Hey—our class, didn't you think there was too much work? There was way too much reading."

"Well, it's an English class."

"Too much reading!"

One of the girls showed Nelda something on her cell, and Nelda laughed. "He's so crazy!" Cell phone girl cackled and bent over the screen, texting away some nonsense or other. Nelda watched her, half smiling, cheerful about something, and then she looked at me.

"So, you finished too, right?"

"Naw—I barely started."

"Travis!" Nelda—a shriek, almost. I sat back. "It's due

tomorrow—you better get to work!"

"Yeah, fuck it." Me. The other girls were all laughing at something—all of them looking at their phones. "The thing is, I'm changing my topic—I might have to take an incomplete."

"That's crazy!" Nelda.

"No, it makes sense."

The waitress brought over the drinks they'd ordered—cocktails, something pale and citrus-y looking.

"To the end of the semester!" Nelda. Everyone—even me—raised their glasses and clinked them, all smiling and happy. Cheers! Well, I guess.

"Drinking games!" The first girl with the phone. Drinking games. Holy shit. Drinking games: I could never understand why people my age couldn't just hang out and get drunk and bullshit around—why getting fucked up had to be turned into a stupid game, had to be hidden, turned into something other than what it was. I think it was maybe the DARE propaganda kicking in again, school-imposed anti-intoxication guilt. People wanted to get loaded, and they were going to get loaded, but they felt guilty about it and tried to turn it into something else—a game. Kids were always wild for the drinking games— one of the reasons I hung around with people older than me.

They agreed on Questions, a game as stupid as any other: One player—it was almost always girls playing Questions, but of course there I was sitting with them—asks a question of another, and the questionee fires a question at someone else, and on and on—but if the questionee laughs or pauses or answers the question, she has to take a drink.

"Brittney." Nelda. "When was the last time you got laid?"

"Whitney." Brittney. "How much are you going to drink tonight?"

"Manda." Whitney. "What'd you do that time you forgot the condoms?"

I drank on every question. Almost bored, and I never get bored—but almost. I looked up and saw Barnes looking at me, shaking his head, disappointed in me. Barnes always told me I was wasting my time with college girls, that I would never get anywhere with them, that I was crazy, that I had nothing to offer—I wasn't handsome, I didn't have money, I didn't have a good job, I didn't have status—I didn't have a life, a normal life, anyway. Barnes said that the only way I could get laid was to concentrate on bored, middle-aged, alcoholic divorcees who were looking for fun, not a boyfriend—and it was true that about the only times I got laid were with women in their thirties or forties who were drunk or crazy or depressed or fucked-up in one way or another, like the woman at the Chili Parlor—which was fine with me.

"Nelda," Jenna said. "Where's the strangest place you've done it?"

"Travis." Nelda. She took a big breath. "*When* are you going to finish that *paper*?"

I paused—I drank.

:::::

Okay. How about:

> On January 1st of this year I witnessed the
> murder of Dwayne Richard Hance, age 21.
> In the time since then I have been trying
> to figure out what it all means and I'm still
> not sure but think it has something to do
> with a narrative of violence. In my paper I
> will compare what happened to me to what
> happened to Donnie in *The Big Lebowski*
> and to Paul in *A River Runs Through It*—I
> think it's what happens after the deaths
> that is more important than the deaths
> themselves, and that is what I will write
> about.

It would have to do, and so I hit the print button and listened to the hounds out front baying at a jogger or something, and then it was time to go.

: : : : :

I was about half-lost when Nelda texted me saying that she was lost for real, and I almost ran off the road reading her text:

hey im lost!!!!!1!!!1

I looked up—death staring me in the face once again, I was heading for some trees—but I dropped the phone and corrected my steering and straightened up and saw Dr. Braddock's street. I pulled in and stopped by the curb and collected my phone and answered Nelda.

**im parked at westlake and her street now
u can prob c my car**

About five minutes later Nelda came along, from the wrong direction, and I guess she saw me and pulled into the street and rolled down her window.

"GPS is a big lie!" Nelda. "I've been driving around out here for hours!"

"All you have to do is listen to it." Me.

"It lies!"

She sped off and I followed her up the street to the end of the cul-de-sac, and I parked in front of Dr. Braddock's house. Nelda circled around a couple of times before stopping on the far side, and she got out of the car carrying a bottle of orange juice. Oh—I remembered then it was a party, and I was supposed to bring chips, and I didn't. Oh well.

"Coming out to her house like this is just so weird." Nelda. She followed me up the path to the house and through the gate. "Did you finish?"

"Got my proposal finished." Me. "Either I get an incomplete or I get nothing."

"You're crazy!"

"Yeah—" I knocked on the door and it popped open, and

Dr. Braddock was there in a cream-colored sweater and jeans and boots, a pair of reading glasses hanging from a cord around her neck, and I could see past her into the front room of the house. Jared was in there, and Jenna the artsy girl, and a couple of the boring girls. There was a nook just off the kitchen, with a table covered with food and whatever—other people brought chips, which was good cover for me, and there were cookies and celery sticks and various gross things that I wouldn't ever eat. Nelda dumped her jug of juice on the counter and grabbed a cookie, and we followed Dr. Braddock into the front room.

"So, you have your papers ready?" Dr. Braddock. She stood in the middle of the room, and I could see a pile of folders on the floor next to the fireplace. Nelda and I were both carrying pocket folders, hers purple, mine dark blue—hers was purple, and it was also sort of thick, a little thick: there was a paper in it. Mine was blue and skinny: all it carried was a one-page—a one paragraph!—proposal, a printout of the tiny newspaper story about Hance's murder, and the few aborted pages of the failed Wm. Henry Jackson paper.

Nelda handed her folder over: I held mine back, looking at Nelda's folder in Dr. Braddock's hand.

"Can I." Me. Choking, almost. Scared, yes. "Can—I talk to you—about my paper?"

Everybody else heard me, of course, Jared and Jenna and the boring girls. Well, fuck them.

"Oh—" Dr. Braddock. "Well, sure."

"Uh, alone?"

Nelda frowned at me, a mocking frown or a supportive frown, I don't know. A frown.

"Sure—let's go up to my office." Dr. Braddock turned and went up the stairs and I followed her, and I could see her boots ahead of me on the stairs: tall and black with green ivy leaves worked into the leather. Her office was the first room on the left, bright sun coming through the window, pictures of Austin and the university all over the walls, not framed pictures, but what looked to be computer printouts—some shots of the south mall, statues, old pictures of parades and football games, street scenes. I stopped in front of an old black and white picture of a tornado—a funnel cloud, at least—hovering over the capitol dome.

"Wow." Me.

"My next project, I think." Dr. Braddock sat in a big soft chair behind her desk and wheeled around to face me. "Austin, the university—how they influence each other, what it means."

Yeah—somehow things always came down to meaning, whatever the fuck meaning means.

"Sit down." Dr. Braddock was watching me.

The only other chair in the room had a big orange tomcat stretched out in it, dozing.

"That's Fred—you can move him."

I scooped the cat up under my arm and sat down in the chair. Fred the cat stayed limp on my lap, began to purr.

"So?" Dr. Braddock. "What's up?"

"Well, I don't have anything for you." Me. Might as well tell the truth. "I want to change my topic—I have a proposal." I offered her the blue folder while I steadied Fred the cat with my other hand.

"You have a proposal." Dr. Braddock stopped. She was kind of half-smiling, maybe. "For a paper that's due *today*— for a paper that's due right *now*."

"Yeah." Me. "I guess I'll have to take an incomplete, too— if I can."

"Okay." Dr. Braddock. She was just looking at me. "So, you don't think you can finish the paper this afternoon?"

"Uh, no."

"How about before I turn the grades in next week?"

She was fucking with me.

And I guess deserved it—yeah, I did. I just shook my head. I leaned forward and dropped the proposal on her desk, and she took it and put her glasses on and looked at it—which took maybe two seconds—and I told her the story: not as much as I'd told Holt, I just told her the important parts, and

Dr. Braddock listened, the big cat stretched out across me.

"Well, the incomplete's not a big deal." Dr. Braddock took her glasses off and let them hang. "It just leaves me with one less paper to grade, and it'll turn into an F automatically if you don't do anything."

"Okay."

"About your proposal." She put her glasses back on, and looked at the sheet of paper for longer than it would take to read it. "You compare what you witnessed—what you experienced—to what happens to Donnie and to Paul in the texts you cite—but they're fictional characters who *died*. Right? And you're real, and you didn't die, so you're not really like them at all. You're not the ultimate victim here."

"Uh." Me, blushing. Why did she always make me blush? "I guess not. No."

"I think you just worded that clumsily." Dr. Braddock. "You might want to take more time and think a bit when you actually write your paper."

"Okay."

"I wonder, though, how you're going to pull this off." Dr. Braddock waited a long time, but I didn't say anything—didn't have anything to say. I was wondering that, too, actually, a little. "It's a big topic, and it could be a really good essay. Or a book, maybe. But the problem you have is something that all young writers have—and I know this because I was once a young writer, too—and that's being shallow."

I sat back as far as I could with the cat on me. The fuck. Shallow? Did she just call me stupid?

"Now, I don't mean that in a negative way—I just mean you can't help it. Young people are—young—they don't have context, or perspective, or experience."

"I'm working on that—" Me. My project. My life!

"Sure! But if you're going to do this right, you're going to have to figure out what it means—what it meant, the death of—" Dr. Braddock looked at the proposal.

"Hance." Me.

"Hance. What his death meant—and means, to you. What

his life meant to him, and to his family. To do it right you'll have to do more than just compare and contrast the event with these two texts. You'll have to think. It's going to be hard, right? It might take years—it might take a lifetime to find the meaning."

I sat there. Back to meaning again. Meant. Fuck. I sat there, didn't say anything.

"But I think you should do it—it just won't be easy."

"Okay." I could still agree with her, she was doing me a favor. And she probably knew more about writing essays—or writing anything—than I did. It was easiest to just sit there and agree with her.

"Yeah?" Dr. Braddock was leaning over the desk toward me. "*Okay* okay?"

"Yeah." Me. Sure, whatever, okay. "Okay."

"Okay!"

We came back down the stairs and Nelda made another face at me—but, you know, I was feeling kind of good, finally, all of a sudden. I'd dodged that bullet—or that knife, or the murderer's fist, or whatever—I'd dodged it, and now I had a year to write the goddamn paper, a year to figure out what it meant, if meant anything.

A couple of the wussy frat boys had arrived, and Dr. Braddock collected their papers. I sat next to Nelda on the saggy couch. Dr. Braddock put the new folders on the pile and then went into the kitchen.

"So?" Nelda, almost a whisper.

"Everybody get something to eat?" Dr. Braddock, from the kitchen. "Or snack on?"

"Incomplete." Me, not whispering.

"Crazy lazy!" Nelda. "Why didn't you just sit down and write it? Or at least pay somebody to write it for you?"

"No—"

Nelda, still whispering. "I know somebody who can write your paper!"

Dr. Braddock came back through carrying a plate covered in plastic, and she went through the room and out onto the deck. There was a big shiny new gas grill out there, and she began putting burgers on to cook.

"So." Dr. Braddock, leaning in the door with a spatula in her hand. "Why don't we get started?"

Everyone sat there, uncomfortable.

"What I'd like you to do." Dr. Braddock. "I'd like you to go around the room, and everyone should talk about something they're taking away from this class. Some memory—it could be from the material we covered, it could be something funny someone said...."

Well. That seemed kind of stupid and touchy-feely. I pushed up out of the couch, tying not to sink back onto Nelda, and I went around the corner to the bathroom and shut the door. Dr. Braddock had a vanilla-scented candle burning in the bathroom, and I turned on the water and ran it while I peed. I looked down, into the corner of the room, and I saw a cat bed there, with a cat in it, an old gray tabby, looking sleepily back at me.

"Hello, cat."

The cat blinked and I flushed the toilet and rinsed off my hands, left the water running in the sink, and dried my hands—and then I brought a little plastic bag out of the change pocket of my jeans, a plastic bag with whitish yellowish powder—crank, of course. I took my car key—the ignition key, hey—and shoveled a key-full up one nostril, then the other, then back to the first for good luck. Yes! Ignited. Keys back to pocket, crank back to pocket:::::and I looked at the cat, looking at me.

"Yes!" Me.

Everything pretty much made sense now, or something did—something. Meaning! Meaning. Meant. I turned off the water and gathered up the cat, and went back out to the living room.

"Uh...." Jenna the artsy girl was talking, trying to talk, watching me come out of the bathroom. "Okay, I remember, like, when you—Travis." She pointed at me, and I stood there with the cat. "You said you wanted to drop a bomb on your parents! That was so funny!"

"I *am* a bomb—I drop myself." Me. I dropped the cat gently onto Nelda's lap:::::and she caught the cat and both of them looked confused. "I think you need a cat."

"And I'll always remember how you came to class hungover all the time."

Everyone laughed at me.

"And we had good discussions, too." Jenna. I guess she liked the class. "There was a lot of freedom!"

"We did have some very good discussions!" Dr. Braddock, from out on the deck. The grill top was open, and thin gray meat smoke was rising toward the sky. A couple of other people were out on the deck, helping her or watching, and I stood there, the bitter crank taste rolling down my throat—wonderful, brilliant, astonishing—and after a moment I stepped out onto the deck to get a soda from an ice chest.

"Nelda?" Dr. Braddock. "It's your turn."

"Uh...." Nelda was still holding the gray cat. She let him flop to the floor, and the cat sat for a minute, looking pissed, and then stalked slowly off, his ears cocked back. "Uh, I guess everybody's already said everything I remember."

"That won't do." Dr. Braddock. "You need to come up with something—just one thing."

"—the movies?" Nelda. "I guess I liked the movies, and I like the pictures we looked at."

"So you liked the visual components of the class?" Dr. Braddock.

"Yeah!"

"I guess that's good enough." Dr. Braddock turned around, faced me, still holding the big spatula in her hand, and I had a quick thought that she might smack me with it. "Travis? You get to finish."

"Fuck, I don't know." I shrugged and tried to think. Think:::::the class, the class:::::kicking idiot Jared out of my special seat had been a triumph, but other than that, all the days, the weeks, the minutes, all the time going by—it all blurred together—words people places——"Everything?"

"C'mon, Travis, saying everything's like saying nothing." Dr. Braddock.

"No—really!" Me. I suddenly knew it *was* everything. "Really—this was a good class. I, uh—liked the readings, the movies—the everything!"

"But what are you going to remember? What one thing are you going to take with you?"

Well, fuck. There really was only everything, even if I had to call it one thing. William Henry Jackson. Dwayne Richard Hance. The murderer. Barnes. Broughton. Chris McCandless. Holt. Carlos. The woman from the Chili Parlor. The hounds. Jail. One thing, and it was everything—all things, and everybody, merged into one great big thing....

"Uh, I don't know." Me. Of course I did know. But how to actually say—everything? "I guess maybe working on that paper I didn't finish?"

"Perfect!" Dr. Braddock. She turned around and flipped a burger. "See, everybody? It's the process that's important. I've been telling students that for years, but none of you ever pay attention. Well, until now."

Almost all my little classmates were sitting around smirking at me like I was a dumbass—loaded, velocitized, with an incomplete—but so what? They'd all die if they tried to do what I did, if they tried to live my life, think my thoughts—and while maybe it was true, like Barnes had said, that most of them didn't *want* to do what I did—that didn't matter, because I was doing it anyway, for them:::::::I was an explorer, a scout, out there, in the night, in the day, jangling, cranked—thinking, yes, this was the way it was—out there on the edge—people everywhere going through their dull dreary daily lives, none of them really caring about anything, all ignorant and lost, and only *I* knew what was really going on—only *I* could see—only——

"Well." Me. Looking at Dr. Braddock. Thinking. Going right now for that one last word or five or ten to end this class, because I had a year to come up with all the other words I might need. A year was a lot of time. A year was a lot of paying attention::::::::::::::::::::A year was a lot of words! Whew. "I guess that's maybe because all those other people don't know enough to fucking care——?"

Acknowledgments

I of course owe a special thanks to Chuck Taylor of Slough Press, for giving this book its first home.

Thanks too to all the other many people who helped along the way: Andrea Bates, Patricia Bjorklund, Pamela Booton, Olivia Burgess, Chris Carmona, Paul Christensen, Phil Gavenda, Alysa Hayes, Larry Heinemann, Kathryn Lane, Jerome Loving, Janet McCann, John McDermott, JeFF Stumpo, Reji Thomas, and Javier VanWisse-Booton. And I gratefully remember all the teachers and students and colleagues who have—in many ways, good and bad—educated me.

About this Edition

One of the questions I had to face as I prepared this new edition was whether I should revise the original text to reflect recent changes in Austin, Texas, the setting of the novel. I faced this on my first novel, too—by the time I finished writing *That Demon Life* and got it published, some of the streets I mentioned actually no longer existed! I was rather puzzled and bummed and worried by this, until my boss at the time, Dr. Charles Henry Rowell, reminded me that I had not written a tourist guidebook to the city, but a *novel.*

So too with *Professed.* In the last year, for example, the University has removed the infamous statue of Jefferson Davis and has placed a monument in remembrance the people shot on August 1, 1966. And, beyond the University, Austin as a whole has continued its decades-long project of transformation and retransformation, emerging seemingly every month as something new and different. But I decided against rewriting the text to keep up with or reflect any of those changes or transformations. *Professed* is a novel about people interacting *with* a place, not a guidebook *to* a place.

LMW

About Lowell Mick White

Lowell Mick White is the author of three books: *That Demon Life* and *Professed*, novels, and *Long Time Ago Good*, a story collection. His work has been published in many literary journals, including *Callaloo*, *Iron Horse Literary Review*, and *Short Story*. A winner of the Dobie-Paisano Fellowship, awarded by the University of Texas at Austin and the Texas Institute of Letters, White received his PhD from Texas A&M University. He was recently inducted into the Texas Institute of Letters.

White can be contacted at www.lowellmickwhite.com

www.ingramcontent.com/pod-product-compliance
Lightning Source LLC
Chambersburg PA
CBHW050409190726
48284CB00007BB/2501